Robert Starnes

Deep dark secrets uncovered by the outsider Detective!

Echoes in Whispering Pines

A Novella

Robert Starnes

Robert Starnes

Published by Starnes Books LLC
Edited by Carpenter Editing Services, LLC
Resources on Childhood Trauma provided by Emma Massey

ISBN: 979-8-9892401-7-3 (sc)
ISBN: 979-8-9892401-6-6 (e)

Printed in the United States of America
First Printing, 2024

Table of Contents

Robert Starnes

Chapter 1
A New Beginning

Detective Brenda Wisely began her first day, as the only detective in Whispering Pines, with thoughts of a fresh start for her and her son. Brenda and her son were leaving a painful life they had in Atlanta, GA. Brenda's husband was killed in the line of duty six months prior to her packing up their life and moving to a small town in Texas. Brenda chose Whispering Pines because it was a small county town with little to no crime. She felt she could start a new life with her fourteen-year-old son, Dalton. Dalton was having a tough time in school after the death of his father. There were accusations of her husband being on the take with the local crime lord. Once those actuations made it to the media Brenda and her son Dalton both were left with ridicule from her fellow officers and by Dalton's classmates. This led to Brenda's decision to take a new job, anywhere but Atlanta. So, she chose Whispering Pines.

Brenda and Dalton moved to Whispering Pines only a few days before she was to begin her new position as the only detective in the small town. Brenda was up to the challenge but was more worried about how the other children would treat Dalton. The day after their move was completed, Brenda took Dalton to Whispering Pines Jr./Sr. High School to make sure he was enrolled. With all the days he missed during his last month in Atlanta, Brenda wanted to make sure he would have enough credits to move up to a sophomore next year. With only six weeks left in the school year, her worries were put to rest after meeting with the school principal, Mr. Barnes. He assured her that Dalton would be able to move up if he did not miss any more days and was able to keep up with the class assignments.

Dalton was able to start his new school the next day, while Brenda focused on getting everything unpacked in their new home. Brenda took time hanging up their family photos all around the house. She wanted to make sure Dalton never forgot his father and who he was. They both know his father was not what everyone was making him out to be. He was a good, honest, loving father and husband. She knew someone was setting up her husband to be a scapegoat for the other corrupt officers in Atlanta, but she had no proof. She was now ready to put those days behind them so they could start again in a peaceful place that did not know of her recent past, or her husband's.

The day passed by as Brenda spent the entire day unpacking, hanging up family photos, and arranging the furniture in every room, including Daltons. She hoped he would appreciate the work she had put in for the day when he got home from his first day of school in Whispering Pines. Once Brenda was satisfied with the outcome of their new home, she decided she wanted to cook an early supper for her and Dalton so she could hear all about his first day at school.

Brenda was still in the kitchen finishing their home cooked meal, she didn't even hear Dalton come into the house from school. Dalton snuck up behind Brenda and gave her a good scare, by goosing her on her sides.

"Dalton! What are you doing sneaking up on me like that? I could have shot you!" Brenda exclaimed with some laughter in her voice.

"Sorry mom. I couldn't resist scaring you. You were just so busy cooking, which is out of the normal for you these days. I thought you may have been replaced by a clone or something," Dalton jokingly replied to his scared mother.

"Okay, you had your fun, now go and wash up for supper," Brenda barked at Dalton. "And don't take too long, I was to hear all about your day today, before the food gets cold!"

"Yes mother," Dalton replied as he turned and walked away, leaving Brenda in the kitchen to finish getting the food ready.

While the food continued to cook, Brenda made her way into the dining room to set the table. She was ready to hear something good come from Dalton today. She had been so worried about how he was handling the stories and news about his father. Brenda wanted him to feel comfortable when he got home. When the table was all set, Brenda went back into the kitchen and took supper off the stove and placed it all on serving platters and placed it all on the table.

With the table set and Brenda sitting alone in the dining room, Dalton came walking in. He really seemed surprised at the spread of food his mom had prepared for them.

"Mom, why did you cook so much food? You know it's just you and I right? How are we going to eat all this?" Dalton inquired of his mom's hard work.

"Dalton, take a seat please, and you could have just said 'Thank you mom,' instead of worrying about how we are going to eat everyone." Brenda suggested it to her only son.

Dalton took his mom's suggestion and took a seat at the table. Dalton began taking small amounts of food from every platter his mother had placed on the table. He was afraid he would upset her more if he didn't at least try a little bit of everything she had spent time, what looked like hours in the kitchen, making. When his plate was overflowing with many of his favorite food, he sat his plate down and began to eat bits and pieces of everything. As Dalton devoured the food off his plate, Brenda sat there quietly, waiting to hear about Dalton's first day of school.

"So, how was your first day of school? Did you make any new friends?" Brenda felt the need to start prying information from her own son.

Dalton took a moment from eating, sat his knife and fork down on his plate and looked at his mother. He wanted to get a feel for what she really wanted to know before answering her questions.

"School was fine, mom. I met several people today, many of course were my teachers, while a few others were classmates. We really didn't have a lot of time today to start building bonding relationships with each other, but who knows what the future holds. Now, can I get back to eating this lovely meal you prepared?" Dalton wasn't really in the mood for talking about school since it was only his first day.

"That is all you have to say about school today? Do you like your classes and teachers at least? Come on, you must tell me more about your day," Brenda pressed Dalton for more information.

"Yes, I like my classes and teachers. They seem to be cool. Apparently, it's not very often that there is a new student that transfers here. From what I gather, most of the students have been going to school together since kindergarten. Several of the teachers are parents of some of my classmates. I am not sure where I will fit in, as most of the students seem to be in some clique or another. But, on the bright side, no one here said anything about dad, which is a plus. It will take a little time for me to find my place, but I believe there is one for me here," Dalton expanded on his thoughts of their new hometown.

Brenda felt a sense of relief that Dalton didn't have to hear anything about his father, and the fact that he believes he can find friends there. Dalton was not a shy kid, but after everything with his father, all his friends stopped talking to him and began talking about him. When all his so-called friends started talking about him pushed him into a shell Brenda thought he would never be able to break free from, but it sounds like he might be able to in Whispering Pines. Hearing what Dalton had just told her gave her the satisfaction of knowing she did the right thing, taking the new job and moving away from the city.

After they finished supper, Dalton excused himself to go to his room so he could work on his homework, to stay on course to move up a grade at the end of the school year. Brenda let Dalton leave the table and took time to clean up the table. As she was cleaning up, she couldn't help but laugh because Dalton was right about all the food. She had no idea she made so much for just one meal, so she had plenty of food left to put in storage containers for them to eat the leftovers for the rest of the week.

It was around seven o'clock when Brenda finished putting all the food away and cleaning up all their dishes in the kitchen. With everything put in the refrigerator, or the dishwasher, Brenda wanted to take a little time for herself. She knew Dalton would be busy the rest of the night in his room doing his schoolwork, so she decided she would take a drive around town. Brenda wanted to get a feel for the town she would be protecting as the only detective in the town. She wanted to see where the local stores were located as well and the sheriff's office she would be working out of. Brenda was used to working in a large city as a beat police officer and then a detective, so moving to a small country town was something new she would have to get used to. Usually by this time of night, Brenda would have been on her third or fourth call, usually involving domestic violence or something involving drugs. But as she drove around Whispering Pines, she could tell her nights would not be so involved with the people.

As Brenda drove around, which only took her about thirty minutes to go down every road, pass every gas station, the supermarket, and her new office, before she was back at home. While she drove around the town, she saw the town was incredibly quiet. The only people out were eating at the local Dairy Queen, or the restaurants on the town square. She did not see any suspicious people walking around, which she was used to, much less anyone disturbing the peace. She was not sure how she would be able to adapt to this new way of life for her. While she was excited to start her new job, she also was worried about being too bored at work that she may not like it. She wondered how she would be able to spread all the free time she was anticipating having when she did start. But she let those thoughts pass and decided to go to bed early, so she would be well rested when she met the Sheriff and other officers she would be working with the next day.

Brenda woke up around five o'clock the next morning, after having a great night's sleep. She had no dreams of the painful life she left behind in Atlanta, or the things that were being said about her husband. She just felt her life was just about to begin with Dalton. Away from all the noise of the city to the quiet life of the country. Brenda jumped out of bed and made her way into the bathroom so she could get cleaned up and ready for her first day. Dalton had his first day the day before, so today was her day and she wanted to make a good first impression on everyone at the Sheriff's office, as well as the town folk.

Once Brenda was ready for work, she went into the kitchen and chose to make breakfast for Dalton, something she rarely had time to do before the move. She made eggs, bacon, and toast and was about to shout out for Dalton to come get breakfast when he came walking into the kitchen.

Dalton was surprised, once again, by his mother's efforts to make their transition easier.

"Wow, supper and now breakfast? I must ask, what have you done with my mother?" Dalton joked to Brenda.

"Oh, be quiet. You may as well get used to this type of behavior from me for now on. I know I was not always available to cook your meals in the past, but that is all about to change. You wait and see. Things will be different for us both here. I have a good feeling about this small town," Brenda expressed to Dalton. "So, eat so you won't be late for school."

"If you insist," Dalton didn't want to disappoint his mother on her first day at work.

Dalton ate his breakfast and told his mother goodbye for the day and wished her luck. Since they only lived a few streets away from the school, Dalton wanted to walk to school, giving Brenda some extra time to clean up after they ate before she had to make her way to work.

Brenda's drive only took her around six minutes to make it to the Sheriff's office, which was about an hour shaved from her time to commute to the precinct in Atlanta, on a good day. Brenda pulled up to the Sheriff's station and parked her car outside on the street in front of the small building. She checked herself out one last time in her car mirror before exiting the car to begin her way into the office. Before Brenda pulled the door open, she took a deep breath to center herself. She didn't want to look nervous when she went inside. She wanted to look professional and ready to work.

Entering the Sheriff's office, Brenda was met by a dispatcher sitting in the front of the office. She was not prepared for just how small the office really was. As she entered, she noticed, behind the dispatcher's desk were two desks. It looked as if it was for two deputies, she assumed it was for two who worked each shift, but she found out later it was only for four deputies to share. They all worked twelve-hour shifts and rotated weekly. Many of the shifts were only covered by only one deputy at a time, so the other could take a day off. Two worked during the day and two worked during the night. The

Sheriff worked during the day of course. Brenda was not sure what her schedule would be yet. When she made it to work, she was there before the Sheriff, or the other officers were in, so she waited at the desk next to the dispatcher, who gave her the ins and outs of the office.

Brenda did not have to wait long before Sheriff Harper came in and introduced himself to Brenda. After their introductions, he had Brenda follow him to his office to inform her of everything going on in Whispering Pines at the time, which was not much at all. There was nothing scheduled for Brenda to work on as a detective yet, so Sheriff Harper decided to put Brenda on cold cases. He felt if she looked over the cold cases, she would get a feel for the dark side of Whispering Pines, which was not actually dark. Brenda was excited to go over their cold cases because many cold cases are solved with a new fresh set up eyes look over them.

Brenda was escorted by Sheriff Harper to a small room at the back which held all the past cases, with only a few of them being cold cases. Once Sheriff Harper left Brenda alone, she walked over to a dusty file cabinet and began to pull out the small number of cold cases Whispering Pines had to offer. After reading the first couple of cases, she felt there was nothing cold about them. She felt those cases could have been solved already, if they didn't involve family members of such people as the mayor, or the Bank Presidents' son. So, Brenda pushed them aside because she did not want to reopen a cold case where everyone already knew who the crime was committed by but chose to not charge the person for the crime for one reason or another. Brand was not ready to step on toes on her first day.

While reading over the cold cases, there was one case which caught her eye. It was a case of a sixteen-year-old child who disappeared without a trace. There were no suspects, no witnesses, or even foul play suggested. Just a report of a missing child who was presumed to have run away, but there was no information regarding the child being found alive, or dead. This was the cold case Brenda felt she wanted to pursue. So, Brenda put all the other cold cases away, back in the dusty file cabinet and focused only on this one case.

Chapter 2

The Cold Case

Brenda sat in the small room Sheriff Harper escorted her to when he first arrived at the station. Brenda read the police report, which was inside the dusty file she found in the stack of cold cases for Whispering Pines and was dumbfounded to find out no one ever followed up on this case. In Atlanta, missing children's cases were worked on for months on end until either a body was found, the child was found alive, or officers ran out of leads. In this case, the file looked as if it had only been worked on for a month, before being considered a cold case. This struck Brenda by surprise.

Brenda read over every statement from classmates, friends, and family so many times she felt she knew the victim. From everything Brenda read about David 'Davie' Youngblood, he seemed like an exceedingly kind and responsible young boy. He had no prior run-ins with the law, did very well in school, and everyone spoke highly of him. Brenda did not understand how anyone could go missing in such a small town, and no one knew anything about what could have happened to Davie. Brenda understood a missing child case with no body, or the child being found alive, murder would be extremely hard to prove, even with a suspect, but Brenda felt so much more could have been done with the case. Brenda wanted to start with the cold case of Davie Youngblood if Sheriff Harper approved.

Brenda picked up all the statements she had read and placed them back in the file, then she tucked the file under her arm and went to find Sheriff Harper. As she made her way from the back of the sheriff's office and back into the bullpen, she was met by an officer. She was not sure if it was the officer on duty, or the one getting off duty, so he introduced herself.

"Good morning. I'm Detective Brenda Wisely, but you can address me as Brenda."

The officer seemed to be taken aback by Detective Wisely's presence.

"Who are you again?" the officer quickly questioned.

Brenda thought she may have some pushback from the officers, since she was a transplant from Atlanta, but she didn't expect them not to know she was going to be working with them.

"My name is Detective Wisely. I just started here, today. I am from Atlanta, Georgia. Didn't Sheriff Harper inform you that I would be working here?" Brenda shot back at the officer.

"Sorry, Detective, I am starting to remember something being said about us having someone new start working here, but I don't listen much to what the Sheriff says during his briefings," the officer casually replied. "I hate to be so short with you, but I just received a report of a possible body being found. I need to get out to the scene."

Brenda understood why the officer was being so short, once she knew what he was about to do.

"Understood officer. Would you like me to help you?" Brenda suggested.

The officer turned away from Brenda and walked away from Brenda and straight out the station door. Brenda thought it would be best to let the officer go alone. She figured he would call her if he needed any help with the body.

Brenda turned and walked into Sheriff Harper's office to touch base with him and let him know she found a cold case she wanted to peruse.

"Sheriff Harper, since you have nothing for me to help you with, I did find a cold case I would like to review. I feel there may have been some things left out of the file and I would like to see what I can find out about the case," Brenda addressed the Sheriff.

"And which case is that, Detective?" Sheriff Harper inquired as he slowly looked up from his desk.

"The case of David Youngblood, Sheriff," Brenda quickly responded.

Sheriff Harper's eyes turned cold looking at Brenda before answering her.

"We looked all over this town and interviewed everyone we could think of during our search for Davie. What do you think you could possibly find that we couldn't?" Sheriff Harper loudly responded to Brenda.

"Sorry, Sir. I am not saying you did not do everything you could in this case, but sometimes fresh eyes on a cold case can come up new avenues to pursue. With your permission, Sir," Brenda thoughtfully responded to the Sheriff.

Sheriff Harper shifted his cold eyes away from Brenda and back down to the papers laying on his desk before answering her.

"You have my permission, but don't get your hopes up. This is a small town, and everyone knows everything about everyone here, except for this case. You may not get the help you are expecting from the residents here in Whispering Pines," Sheriff Harper ended their conversation and quickly ushered Brenda to leave his office.

Brenda took notice of how the Sheriff was taken back by her suggestion of investigating the case of David Youngblood, which made her believe she may be on to something. Brenda decided to take the file home with her, so she could work away from the eyes of the other officers, including Sheriff Harper.

Brenda told the dispatcher she was going out for a bit and to let the Sheriff know if he needed her for anything to just radio for her. Once the dispatcher had all Brenda's contact information, Brenda walked out of the station and made her way back to her car. With the case file sitting in the passenger seat of her car, Brenda drove off and headed home.

The ride home only took a few minutes from the Sheriff's station, since she only lived three streets past the town square. When she arrived at home, Brenda noticed someone was walking away from her front door. She knew it was not her son, Dalton, as he was at school, so the person who had just left her front porch interested her. Brenda quickly parked her car and quickly exited her car and began to yell at the mysterious person.

"Excuse me, but are you looking for someone?" Brenda yelled out to the unknown person who was previously on her front porch.

A middle-aged woman turned around and looked at Brenda for a moment.

"I'm sorry, are you speaking to me?" the woman replied.

"Yes, I am speaking to you. You were on my front porch when I was pulling up, so is there something I can do for you?" Brenda quickly asked the woman.

"Oh, yes. Sorry, I am your neighbor and wanted to introduce myself, but when I knocked on your door and no one answered I thought I would try again later. If you are busy, I can come back later," Brenda's neighbor responded.

"Please forgive my outburst. I am not used to a neighbor making their way over to my housing to introduce themselves to me. Now is a wonderful time, would you like to come in for a minute?" Brenda apologetically responded to the neighbor.

"Thank you, I would love to come in," the neighbor replied to Brenda.

Brenda walked back over to her car to retrieve the file she had sat in her front passenger seat, before closing the car door and locking it. With the file in hand, Brenda walked back over to her neighbor, who was waiting for Brenda at the end of the sidewalk which led to her front door. Once the two of them were on the sidewalk, Brenda motioned for her new neighbor to follow her to the house.

When they were standing outside the front door, Brenda pushed her house key into the door lock and twisted it until it unlocked the door. With the door unlocked, she pushed the door open and made entry into her home with her neighbor in tow.

"Make yourself at home. Would you like a glass of tea or something to drink?" Brenda asked her guest as she placed the file, which she had in her hand, down on the coffee table before walking towards the kitchen.

"A glass of tea would be great, thank you. My name is Joy."

"It's nice to meet you Joy, my name is Brenda. I am the new detective here in Whispering Pines."

"I know who you are. Everyone in Whispering Pines knows who you are. And your son's name is Dalton. You are both from Atlanta, right?" Joy replied to Brenda.

"How do you know all that? We have only been in town for a few days?" Brenda questioned Joy.

"It's a small-town thing. Everyone seems to know everything about everyone in a small town. When word got out a new, big city detective was about to start working here, people started talking, and the next thing we know is you are here. And of course, since I am your neighbor, I wanted to be the first person to welcome you to Whispering Pines."

Brenda was a little taken back about all the information Joy already knew about her and her son.

Brenda knew it was a small town, but she never expected news to travel that fast.

Brenda continued to make a glass of tea for her guest before making her way back to the living room. As Brenda walked into the room, she noticed Joy was looking at the file she had placed on the coffee table. Brenda handed Joy the glass of tea and quickly grabbed the file and moved it to her desk in the other room before conversing more with Joy.

"Well, Joy, it seems you all know a lot about me, and my son and I know nothing about anyone here in Whispering Pines."

"Small town gossip is a real thing. Nothing goes on in a town this small without someone knowing about it. Once one person knows about it, then everyone knows about it in a matter of days. It can be a good thing, or a terrible thing, depending on how you look at it."

"I am beginning to see that," Brenda made a soft laugh with her reply.

"So, I see you're looking into the Davie Youngblood case again. Is there a reason you are looking into it?" Joy quickly changed the subject.

"Excuse me?" Brenda shot back at Joy.

"I was not trying to be nosey, but the file you have on the coffee table was labeled 'David Youngblood,' so

I figured you must be working on the case. It has been many years since he disappeared. Why are you looking into it now?" Joy questioned Brenda.

"If you are here to get more gossip for the rumor mill, you have come to the wrong place. I do not talk about work with anyone except people at work. So, if that is all you wanted to know, I must ask you to please leave. I have some things to do," Brenda quickly reprimanded Joy.

Joy was taken back by Brenda's behavior, as being from the small town, she had never met such a direct tone before from anyone.

"Again, I am sorry if you think that is why I am here. I can assure you it is not the reason I came over. I genuinely wanted to introduce myself and welcome you to Whispering Pines. But if you ever want to talk about Davie, please feel free to ask me anything," Joy apologized to Brenda for being so forthcoming with her questions.

"No, I'm sorry. I am not used to being confronted by a neighbor, much less one from a small town that likes to gossip. But, since you brought it up, is there anything you can tell me about Davie? Something that may not be in the file?" Brenda decided to take advantage of the situation with Joy.

"Well, you didn't hear this from me, but I heard Davie ran away because of his home life, but then I heard he was taken away from his mother by some relatives up north. I don't know why he was taken away, or who knows the truth, but those are just rumors," Joy openly reported to Brenda.

"And do you believe the rumors?"

"Well, I don't believe everything I hear around this town, and you shouldn't either. Some of the residents here in Whispering Pines are known for giving others inaccurate information just to stir the pot, if you know what I mean," Joy concluded with her assessment of the townsfolk.

Before Brenda could respond to Joy, she received a call on her radio from the dispatcher.

"Detective Wisely, you are needed to assist officer Colton with the possible 10-54 out in Klienstown," the dispatcher relayed to Brenda.

"10-4, let Officer Colton know I'm on my way. Can you send me directions to his location to my cell," Brenda ended her transmission to dispatch.

Brenda looked over at Joy and politely asked her to leave, without letting her know what she was responding to or where she was going. Brenda did not want to give any information to Joy for the rumor mills. Once Joy left Brenda's home, she put her cold case file in her desk drawer and left home to find Officer Colton in Klienstown.

Before Brenda was able to get into her car, her phone let her know of a new text, which she figured was from dispatch, giving her the location of the scene she was going to. Upon reading the text and putting in the GPS location into her phone, she knew she had a drive ahead of her. Klienstown was around twelve miles East of Whispering Pines, with few street signs. Brenda drove down Country Club Road, then hit a highway for a few seconds, before turning onto another road that led to Klienstown. As Brenda drove down a County Road off the highway, it took her another eight minutes before she found the dirt road which would lead her to Office Colton's location. She continued down the dirt road until she was able to see Officer Colton's cruiser.

Brenda pulled up behind the other cruiser, parked her car, and got out to meet Officer Colton.

"What do we have here Officer?" Brenda quickly asked.

Officer Colton looked at Detective Wisely with a pale face and explained to her he had never seen a dead body, much less skeletal remains, which was the case here, before and needed her aid. Brenda acknowledged his need for help and made her way over to where the skeletal remains were lying on the ground. As she arrived at the remains, she was met by Henry Brown, a hunter who found the skull at first.

"Hello, Sir. My name is Detective Wisely, and I will be helping in this investigation. May I ask your name?" Brenda prodded.

"My name is Henry, and I found the bones in my well."

"May I ask what you were doing out here and how exactly did you find the bones?" Brenda started her investigation quickly.

"You see, this is my land and I hunt deer out here. I was making my rounds checking my deer feeders and I heard something coming from the well over there, so I went to see what it could be. When I got there, I noticed one of my calves had fallen in, so I went and got a rope so I could pull it out. When I was able to get the rope around it and was able to pull it up, I noticed there was something else in the rope with my calf. After I got the calf out and it was safe on land, I saw what looked like a human skull on the ground. That was when I called the Sheriff's office for aid," Henry explained to Detective Wisely.

"Thank you, I will need to get your information in case I have any further questions for you, but for now, you may leave," Detective Wisely informed Henry, who had no problem leaving the scene.

After Henry left, Detective Wisely called for the city coroner to come out and retrieve the remaining skeletal bones from the well. Brenda asked Officer Colton to stay at the scene until the remains were removed and to tape off the area around the well. She wanted to make sure the area was preserved in case she needed to go back for a more thorough inspection.

With the scene being taped off and the coroner on her way, Brenda left and went back to the station to fill out her report and inform Sheriff Harper what her preliminary thoughts were about the skeletal remains found on Mr. Browns land.

Robert Starnes

Chapter 3

Ghost of Whispering Pines

The next morning, Brenda received a text from the coroner's office, letting her know they know the identity of the remains found the day before. She called the coroner and found out the skeletal remains found were those of David Youngblood. The news of it being Davie's remains sent shockwaves through her body. Her first day as the town's Detective had led her to the remains of the same cold case she was preparing to work on.

Now with the remains of David Youngblood being identified, Brenda was prepared to do whatever she needed to do to the answers the earlier investigation was unable to uncover. She knew it was not going to be an easy task, retrieving information from a small town, especially when everyone supposedly knew everything about everyone. All the training Brenda had as a Detective, she knew everyone had secrets and rarely enjoyed them being outed, so pushback was nothing new to her. After reading the statements of everyone interviewed during the first investigation, she had a feeling that the best person to speak to about Davie was the teachers at the school, those who should have known him best.

Without informing Sheriff Harper of her plan of investigation, Brenda made her way to the school to begin interviewing the teachers. From what Brenda had learned so far, most of the teachers at the school had been teaching there for many years, many of them taught Davie over the years before his disappearance. Upon arrival at school, Brenda parked her cruiser outside the front of the elementary school. She wanted to start with the teachers who knew Davie when he was young, before middle school or high school drama could have appeared in his life.

Brenda walked into the schools' front doors and headed to the Principal's Officer, which was just in the front as she entered. Walking through the school doors, seeing all the artwork hanging on the walls from the students reminded Brenda of when Dalton was in elementary school, except in Atlanta, their schools did not put artwork for parents to see, they did not do many activities with the students, being overcrowded at the time. Brenda softly smiled to herself, wishing Dalton could have gone to a small school like this one when he was younger, until she reached the office doors.

Brenda entered the Principals Officer and was at once greeted by the school secretary.

"Good morning, Officer Wisely, what can I do for you?"

"Good morning, and it's Detective Wisely," Brenda sternly replied.

"My apologies Detective, sometimes misinformation gets around town before the truth is revealed. I am Ms. Parks, the school secretary. How may I help you?"

"No need to apologize, we just met. Now, I am investigating a cold case here in Whispering Pines, and would like to know if any teachers who taught David Youngblood still taught at the school?" Brenda quickly replied, without giving too much information away for the rumor mill to continue.

Ms. Parks' smile left her face and she looked away from Detective Wisely very quickly. As if she knew of the case.

"Is there something wrong, Ms. Parks?"

"No Detective, it is just that even though Davies' disappearance happened so long ago, it still brings up memories from the past. Not all good memories. When Davie disappeared, the town was in shock. It took years for many residents to get back to their normal routines," Ms. Parks sadly responded to Brenda.

"Really, would you like to elaborate more on that?" Detective Wisely pushed for more information.

"No, sorry. Let me get a printout of the classes and teachers Davie had when he attended here. It will only take a minute," Ms. Parks quickly changed the subject away from herself.

Brenda watched as Ms. Parks walked over to the office computer and began typing away, not saying another word. Brenda thought she could come back later to press Ms. Parks for more details if it was called for but for the moment, she was only interested in speaking to Davies' teachers. She wanted to get a feel for the victim, not gossip.

After five minutes, Ms. Parks turned away from the computer and walked over to the printer and picked up the classes and teachers for Davie. When his schedules were in her hand, she walked back over to Detective Wisely and handed them over.

"If you have everything you need from me, I really do need to get back to work. I have some grades to upload to our system for parents to review," Ms. Parks said to the Detective and without waiting for a reply, turned, and walked back over to her computer.

Brenda looked over the papers Ms. Parks handed her and was able to learn which teachers taught Davie and what rooms they were teaching in now. Without pressing Ms. Parks any further, Brenda thanked her and walked out of the office, back into the school hallway.

Brenda's thought process was not to speak to every teacher at first. She wanted to speak to a few different teachers, in different grades and if anything came up during her interviews, she knew she could revisit the other teachers if needed. Right now, she just wanted some baseline information about Davie. Brenda walked down the hallway to classroom number three. It was the room of a first-grade teacher who taught Davie, Mrs. Ingram.

Brenda investigated the classroom, through a small window in the door, and noticed the class was empty of students, but Mrs. Ingram was in the room sitting at her desk. Brenda knocked on the door before entering, which startled the teacher.

"Mrs. Ingram, I presume?" Brenda inquired as she entered the room.

"Yes, I am Mrs. Ingram, and who may you be?"

"Sorry to interrupt your work, but I am Detective Wisely. I am new to Whispering Pines and I am working on a cold case and want to know if you could assist me on some background information about the victim?" Brenda asked straightforwardly.

"A cold case, here in Whispering Pines? Sounds serious. I will do what I can to help you, but I am not sure if I would be able to provide you with anything you don't already know about the victim. I presume you have the police reports and statements made during the time of the incident," Mrs. Ingram quickly responded.

"You are correct. I do have the report and all the statements, but I am trying to get a better feeling of who the victim was when he was alive. You, being one of his teachers years ago, you may have some insight which was left out of the reports."

"If you insist, who is the victim we are speaking of?"

"His name is David Youngblood. Does the name ring any bells?"

"Oh, I see. You are working on the Davies case. He was such a sweet child, I never thought he would just run away like he did. Everyone loved Davie here in Whispering Pines. So, when he disappeared it shocked the entire town."

"Yes, I am reviewing Davies' cold case file. May I ask, why do you suspect Davie ran away?"

"Well, I heard he ran away and since there was nothing to prove otherwise, we all feel he just ran away."

"There must have been something to make people think that, and if Davie was liked by everyone here in Whispering Pines, why would he just run away? Did anyone ever think something tragic may have happened to him? What do you think could cause a boy to run away like you thought Davie did, you must have thought he had a reason to leave town," Brenda began to question Mrs. Ingram in a way to suggest she knew more than she was letting on.

Mrs. Ingram took a moment to sit and think about how she was going to answer Detective Wisely's questions moving forward and Brenda noticed.

"Mrs. Ingram, I am not here to reopen old wounds of the town, but this boy deserves answers, don't you agree? He was just a child, a child you knew and taught in school, in this classroom I assume. It is your responsibility to help this child, even if it is not pleasant to say. I am here for Davie," Brenda replied in a subtle manner, pleading with her love for children to help Davie.

"Detective Wisely, you must understand, there is only so much a teacher can do for a student. I have lived here my entire life and even went to this same school. While Davie was a student here in elementary school, he WAS loved by all. He was such a pleasant young man and was a teacher's dream student. I will tell you this, you are looking in the wrong school. If you want to find out who Davie was when he disappeared, you need to speak to his high school teachers. High school was when things changed for Davie. Please don't tell anyone I told you that, it would cost me my job, and my reputation in this town," Mrs. Ingram pleaded with Brenda for her discretion.

"Thank you, Mrs. Ingram, I do have one more question for you. Can you think of anyone, other than his high school teachers, I should also be speaking to?"

Mrs. Ingram shuttered before answering Detective Wisely's question.

"I would also speak to the students who were attending high school when Davie did. I knew Davie was having a challenging time in high school but did nothing to help him. He was being bullied by everyone in the school when he disappeared. It was as if everyone he knew and went to school with for years turned on him for some reason or another. I feel horrible for not doing anything to help him during his time of need, so when I heard he ran away, I was relieved. I felt he did not have to deal with the bullies anymore and thought he was living a much happier life," Mrs. Ingram confessed to Brenda, which turned Brenda's stomach. A teacher knowing something is happening to a student and ignores the issues until the child is missing.

"Thank you, Mrs. Ingram. I will be discreet about our conversation today, unless I consider this conversation is pertinent to solve the case and close it," Brenda wanted to protect Mrs. Ingrams honestly, but her priority was to find out who killed Davie.

Detective Wisely thanked Mrs. Ingram for her honesty and left her classroom. Brenda walked along the hallway of the elementary school, scanning the artwork from the students again but this time thinking of how a child's life could change so fast from elementary school to high school. I imagined some of the hanging artwork was Davies at one point in time and how his artwork was not enough to keep him out of harm's way as he got older. Brenda began to rethink her thoughts of Dalton going to a small town after hearing what Mrs. Ingram had to say about Davies so-called childhood friends turning on him the way they did only a few short years of elementary school. Brenda pushed those thoughts aside as she exited the school and walked back to her cruiser. She felt she should take Mrs. Ingrams advice and skip the rest of Davies' elementary teacher as well as his middle school teachers. It was time for her to go straight to the last teachers who had Davie when he disappeared.

Brenda left the elementary school parking lot and made her way down the street to the high school. Brenda was worried she may embarrass her son at school, so he decided to park away from the entrance this time. Brenda knew what classes Dalton was taking and what time they started and since she arrived at the high school only a few minutes before Dalton's next class, she decided to wait in her car until she knew the halls would be empty before entering the building. Once Brenda knew the halls would be clear, she exited her cruiser and made her way to the front entrance of the high school.

As Brenda entered the school, she could see school lockers for the students, which surprised her because she could see some were decorated for a student's birthday, or even some were decorated for the football team. There may not have been artwork hanging on the walls of this school, but she could still see the pride the students had for their school and friends. She just hoped Dalton was really enjoying school like he told her he was.

Brenda made her way down the hallway to the administrative offices of the high school. She hoped she was not greeting the same way as Ms. Parks had greeted her at the elementary school, but her hopes were dashed as soon as she walked into the office.

"Good morning, Detective Wisely, what can I do for you today?" another school secretary announced as she walked in.

"Good morning, as you may already know, I am working on a cold case of a former student who attended here before going missing. So, can you please print out the schedules and teachers he had when he was a student here? His name is…" Brenda was cut off by the secretary.

"Davie Youngblood, correct? It's a small town, as you may have heard, so when you asked for information at the elementary school, we were informed you may be stopping by here as well. I took the liberty of printing out your request so when you arrived you would have everything you need to continue your investigation. Here are the class schedules and teachers list he had here before he ran away. My name is Ms. Carter, and I am the school secretary for the high school. If you need anything, please don't hesitate to ask."

"Thank you, Ms. Carter, can you point me any teacher who may have a free period at this time, one who also taught Davie?"

"Of course, that would be Mr. Stillman. He teaches algebra and has done so for over twenty years here. His room is down the East hallway, room number 107," Ms. Carter pointed out of the office to the hallway Brenda needed to go down to room 107.

Brenda thanked Ms. Carter before turning away from her to exit the office. She didn't look back as she walked away down the East hallway. Brenda was eager to speak to Mr. Stillman, so she didn't pay much attention to the décor of the rest of the school. She continued to walk down the hallway until she reached room 107 and to her surprise, the classroom door was open. Brenda gazed into the room and saw a fit, middle-aged, man with salt and pepper hair sitting at his desk. She was taken back by how young the teacher of twenty years looked. Brenda took a moment to collect herself before knocking on the open door to get Mr. Stillman's attention.

The knocking on the door did not seem to surprise Mr. Stillman, as if he was expecting the new Detective.

"Excuse me, are you Mr. Stillman?" Brenda casually inquired.

"Yes, but you can call me James, only my students call me Mr. Stillman."

"Well, James, I hate to interrupt your free period, but I am sure you already know why I am here. I am Detective Wisely, and I am reviewing a cold case of a past student of yours," Brenda quickly responded to James' offer.

"Yes, I am aware of who you are and why you are here. I would be more than happy to tell you anything I remember about Davie."

"Great, do you mind if I sit down?" Brenda shyly asked James.

"Please, have a seat. Now, what would you like to know about Davie?"

"Well, it's not really about what I want to know about Davie, but more about his friends."

"What do you mean? I thought you were here to get insight on who Davie was, not his friends," James began to shuffle paperwork on his desk as he replied to Detective Wisely.

"It is true I would like to get more background information on Davie, but right now I am more interested in what happened between Davie and his friends when they got to high school? You see, I know more than you may think already about Davie, so I want to know more about his time here in high school and the people he hung around with. Can you help me with any insight on those relationships?" Brenda noticed James was not eager to talk about other students, or their relationships with Davie growing up.

"I'm not quite sure what you are trying to get at? Davie was a fine student here and everyone loved having him as a student. What more do you think I may know about his friendships?" James quickly tried to shut down Brenda's line of questioning.

"I assume, since you have been a teacher here for over twenty years, you would have knowledge of how the students really felt about other students. Did Davie do something to a student, or students, that would change the way his childhood friends felt about him?" Brenda was not about to ease Mr. Stillman's conscience by changing her questions.

"Look, Detective, I am only a teacher here. I am not here to listen to high school drama or rumors. I am here to teach these children algebra and not get into their personal lives. I hope you can respect that?" Mr. Stillman loosely responded, trying to avoid having knowledge of any issues Davie may have had with other students.

Brenda could tell James was holding back. There was something on his mind he didn't want to reveal to Brenda, but she knew how to get information out of suspects, where or not they wanted to let it out.

"James, I know you are not just a teacher for these children, you are also a role model for them. Meaning, you would not want your students to lie to you, just like I don't like it when someone I am just questioning lies to me. I am trying to close this cold case and you may be able to give me other leads to pursue if you are honest with me. Can you do that? If not for me, but for Davie?" Brenda began pulling at Mr. Stillman's pride for more details.

James took a deep breath before responding to Detective Wisely's request.

"Look, Detective, I am not here to try and get anyone in trouble, but what happened with Davie was over ten years ago. The students who attended school then and not the same people they are today. Every school has a child who may be bullied, which in this case was Davie. Yes, there were many rumors going around about Davie changing over the summer before high school and some of the students didn't like how he had changed. They may have expressed how they felt about it, but it was all just talk. Nothing happened to Davie in my classroom, if anything was going on with him and other students, it was either in the hallways or after school. But like I said, it was all just talk. You know how kids are, one minute they are friends with someone and the next minute they are fighting. There was nothing I could have done to change that. Is that what you are waiting to hear?" James' words spit through his teeth like fire as he finished.

Brenda was not too thrilled to hear that a veteran teacher of at least ten years, at that time, was able to ignore signs of a child being bullied and allowed it to happen. If she was not on duty and doing her job, she would have had some unpleasant words to say to James herself, but she resisted the urge to speak her words aloud. She was there for Davie, not her own disapproval of his tactics at the time. Brenda brushed off his words and went back to focusing on who was bullying Davie at the time.

"Mr. Stillman, thank you for being honest with me, now can you tell me the names of the students who bullied Davie? Again, I am just trying to close this case,

I am not here trying to get anyone in trouble or judge their actions. I'm looking for justice for Davie, I hope you can understand," Brenda choked back at what she really wanted to say to Mr. Stillman and gave a professional response to his rhetoric.

James was looking defeated after Brenda asked her last question, as if he knew he should have done something at the time and felt guilty for not trying to help Davie then.

"I can't remember all their names, but I would start by speaking with his best friend before high school. His name is Christopher Wooden, and I am not saying anything more about it. If you don't mind, I have a class about to start soon and I need to prepare today's lesson. You can see your way out," Mr. Stillman expressed content to Brenda, who knew she was not going to get anything more from James right then, so she excused herself and left his room.

Brenda made her way back through the East hallway until she was back at the school entrance. Brenda did not like what she was hearing about Davie, leading up to his disappearance from the teachers. As she walked to her car, she wondered what could have changed in a child over a summer to make all his lifelong childhood friends turn on him in such a drastic manner. What could Davie have done to deserve being bullied to the extent of him being murdered? Brenda wondered before she started her cruiser to head back home to do some more digging into the case.

Robert Starnes

Chapter 4

June's Hope

The next day, Brenda thought it was time she spoke to Davie's mother, June Youngblood. If anyone knew of how a person changed over a summer, I would be their mother. Brenda waited until Dalton left for school before she left to head over to June's home. She wanted to be home for Dalton in case he wanted to talk about anything before going to school, but she was disappointed. Dalton had nothing new to tell her about school or the students, which gave her peace and at the same time, worried her. She wanted to make sure Dalton knew she was there if he needed anything, or just wanted someone to talk to. She didn't want Dalton to end up like Davie.

Brenda was not surprised to learn June still lived in the same home when Davie was alive. Brenda would learn soon enough as to why she still lived there. From Brenda's experience with grieving parents, when their child went missing, or was found dead, they would usually move out of the home they shared with their child. Usually there were too many memories of the missing, or passed, child for the parents to continue living in the same place, but June was a different story, as she would soon find out.

Brenda drove out to a small town, just outside of Whispering Pine, called Ellis. A town so small it only had about eighty-eight residents year-round. The town only had a post office and no other stores. Whispering Pines was only a ten-minute drive from Ellis, since it was only five miles from the town square. As Brenda rode through the small town towards June's home, she never knew just how small a town could be. While Whispering Pines may be considered a small town, Ellis was so small, she wondered how it was even called a town. There was only one road in and out of the town with nothing but a few houses lining the street on either side. Brenda took in the scenery before coming to the end of the road, which stopped at June and Davie's home.

Brenda parked her car and as she exited her car, she was met by several small friendly dogs and several cats. Not really a place Brenda was used to visiting in the past, but still a pleasant place. She continued past all the animals and made her way to the front porch of the home she was visiting.

Brenda knocked on the front door and before she knew it, she was being greeted by a friendly, bubbly person.

"June, I presume," Brenda said.

"Yes, I am June, may I help you?"

"Yes ma'am, I am Detective Wisely with Whispering Pines Sheriff Office, I was wondering if I could speak with you. It's about your son's disappearance ten years ago?" Brenda replied to June with a soft voice.

"So, you are the new Detective? It's nice to see a fresh face around these parts. I'm sorry to tell you, but Davie is not home right now. I'm sure he will be home anytime soon, if you would like to wait with me," June asked Brenda.

Brenda knew right away the reason June never moved was because she still felt Davie was still alive and would come home one day. It pained Brenda to know she would be the one to have to inform June, Davie would never be coming home the way she expected him to. But he would be coming home, for the last time.

"Yes, I would love to sit and speak to you, while we wait for Davie to come home. Do you mind if I come in for a spell?" Brenda softly asked June, not wanting to just blurt out the truth about Davie.

"Please, come on in. I could pour us some tea, if you are thirsty," June responded to Brenda with some southern hospitality.

"Thank you, I would love some tea," Brenda cordially accepted June's offer.

Brenda made her way inside the home and June escorted her to the living room sofa, so June could excuse herself to go to the kitchen to get the tea she promised her guest. As Brenda sat on the sofa, she began to look around at all the photos June had up in the home. There were photos of June and Davie all over the place. One thing Brenda noticed was there were no photos of Davies' father. Brenda had not heard much about Davies' home life since she started reviewing his case. She began to wonder if Davies' father left because of the incident or was he in the picture before he vanished. She felt she would know when the time was right for her to ask June about Davies' father, but she knew it would not be at the beginning of their meeting.

As Brenda continued to look around at the photos on the walls, June snuck into the living room holding two cups of sweet tea for them to enjoy as they waited for Davie to come out. Brenda accepted a glass of tea and thanked June again for the tea and the company.

"June, may I ask you a couple of questions about Davie, before he gets home?"

"You may ask anything you want to know about Davie. He's such a sweet kid, everyone loves him. What would you like to know," June was ready to talk about Davie, and Brenda could tell.

"Thank you, June. What can you tell me about Davies' friends? I've heard everyone loves Davie, but I have not heard much about who his friends are," Brenda eased into the questioning with June.

"Davie has so many friends, I would not know where to start. You see, Davie has gone to school with all his friends since they started kindergarten. He really doesn't claim one friend is more of a friend than another. He really loves all his friends. Why do you ask?" June happily replied.

"I am just trying to get a feel for how his friends treat him. Being such a loving person can sometimes lead to disagreements. Do you know if Davie has any disagreements with any of his friends?"

"Davie has never had a disagreement with anyone. He gets along with everyone."

"I can tell. Everyone in town has nothing but wonderful things to say about Davie. It's so rare for someone to like everyone and be liked by everyone at the same time. How is Davie able to keep such friendships, ones with no disagreements? It must be hard for him at times," Brenda began to press on for more details about Davies' friends, without pushing June into regression.

"I am not sure what you mean. Davie is just one of those people who you can't help but you like. He does great in school and around the house. He helps the folks at church when they need some work done around their houses. He is a very accepting person, never judges people for their mistakes, or life choices. He is just an all-around likable kid."

"He sounds like a good friend to have. Do you know his best friend Christopher Wooden? I hear they were best friends throughout elementary and middle school, until the summer before high school," Brenda prodded June to narrow down who she wanted to know more about.

"Who? I don't think I recognize the name. Like I said before, Davie has tons of friends, I can't remember all their names," June began to shut down after Brenda mentioned Christophers name for some reason. Brenda knew there had to be more to it, so she began to press on.

"You know, Christopher. From what I hear, they spent a lot of time together growing up, until the summer before high school. I'm sure he came here more than once, since they were best friends," Brenda pressed June.

"I don't know who you are talking about, do you mind if we talk about something else? I don't want to be talking about Davies' friends when he gets home. I don't think he would like me talking about his friends to a stranger when he comes home," June shut completely down after Brenda's second attempt to gather more information about Christopher. Brenda knew she could not get anything about Christopher from June, so she needed to go to the source himself later. Brenda decided to change her tactic to find out more about Davie from June.

"Sorry, yes, do you mind if we talk more about Davie? I would like to get to know more about him before he comes home. If that is all right with you," Brenda started speaking in a softer voice again.

"Of course, what do you want to know about my Davie?"

"Do you know if Davie had a girlfriend? I'm sure a sweet lovable boy like Davie must have had his pick of lovely girlfriends," Brenda began to talk Davie up as a lady's man, most mothers loved to hear things like this about their boys.

"Now that you mention it, no, I don't think Davie has a girlfriend. He has always been too polite to ask a girl out. I know the girls just love him though. Girls call here all the time for Davie, either about schoolwork or to see what he may be up to on the weekends."

"I see, I bet he is loved by them all. Can I ask another question about Davie?"

"Sure," June quickly replied, she loves talking about Davie.

"I heard from one of his friends at school that the summer before high school, Davie changed. They of course would not tell me how he changed, but it was a noticeable change in him. Do you by any chance know what they may be talking about? Did you notice a change in Davie during that summer?" Brenda was afraid the mention of the summer before high school would shut June down again, and she was right.

"I have no idea what you could be talking about. The only thing I can think of is that summer Davie got taller, and his voice got deeper. You know, the change when a young boy becomes a young man," June said with pride, feeling her little boy turned into a man that summer.

"I know what you mean. I recently went through that change with my son, Dalton. He is a sophomore at Whispering Pines this year. He felt so awkward the summer his change started, and while he still may be growing, he will always be my little boy," Brenda conveyed to June to show support in understanding what she saw in his change that summer.

"So, when do you think Davie will be home? How long has he been away from home?" Brenda decided it was time to start bringing June around to the present.

"He has not been gone long. I am expecting him back at any time. Why do you ask?" June looked over at Brenda with a sad look in her eyes.

"No reason, I was just wondering. I was looking at all the photos you have of you and Davie, but I noticed there are none of his father. May I ask where Davies' father is?"

"Davies' father left us many years ago. Davie and his father did not get along very well, so when he left, I took it as a sign. We are better off without him being around. He was very abusive to Davie growing up. He would call him nasty names when he was a small child. It was just too much for either of us to handle, so when he left, we counted our blessings," June had no problem speaking ill of her ex-husband, so Brenda thought she should keep on the subject.

"That sounds awful. What could make a father do such things to their own child? Do you mind me asking, what things did he say to Davie?" Brenda pressed on.

"They were horrible things. He would call Davie vulgar words, like 'faggot' 'queer' and sometimes a 'sissy.' No child should ever have to hear their father call them those things, no matter how sweet the child is. Davie was extremely sensitive growing up, until his father left. That was when Davie broke out of his shell and became the perfect son. His father didn't break

Davie and I know nothing will break him now. He has had no issues since his father left," June spouted out to Brenda with disdain in her voice of the words his father chose to use to call him.

Brenda wanted to ease June's pain from Davies' father, but the only way she could do that was to be honest with June right then. It was time she told June Davie never left her, he was taken away from her too soon.

"June, there is another reason I wanted to stop by today to meet with you. I know this is going to be extremely hard to hear, but there is something I need to tell you about Davie," Brenda began to ease June into hearing the truth about where Davie was.

"No, you can't say anything to me about Davie. I know he will be home soon, you wait and see," June stopped Brenda from finishing her sentence. It was as if June already knew when Brenda was about to tell her, but she was not ready to hear it.

"I'm so sorry to have to tell you this, June, but Davie is not going to be coming home today like you think. Davies' remains was found yesterday in Klienstown. His skeletal remains were discovered down inside a well on a hunter's land. The remains were positively identified as David Youngblood by his dental records by the coroner. Again, I am so sorry to inform you of this news, but you will be able to bring Davie home to be placed at rest finally. That should give you some comfort," Brenda expressed to June, as June sat there crying uncontrollably of the news.

June felt deep down inside Davie did not run away, but she never imagined he would never come home again. Once June was able to compose herself, she had to ask Brenda a question.

"Did he take his own life?" June questioned.

"Why would you think such a thing? No, from the preliminary autopsy findings, Davie was murdered. We do not know who killed Davie, or why, but I want you to know that I will do everything in my power to find out who took Davie away from you and bring justice to his killer. You have my word," Brenda promised June, and she intended to keep her promise. "May I ask why you asked if Davie took his own life? What would give you the impression he could have done something like that?"

"I may not have been completely honest with you before, but Davie did change during the summer before high school. Davie came out to me that summer and said he wanted to be honest with his friends and wanted to come out to them as well. I, of course, tried to talk him out of coming out to his friends that early. That was something personal to him and his friends didn't need to know about it. I knew they would not like it if he came out to them. You see, Whispering Pines is not known for being an accepting town. The town has always been full of judgmental people and strong religious beliefs, so being gay in Whispering Pines was not something the residents would never accept. I knew if Davie came out to his friends, then their parents would soon know as well. I knew once their parents found out, they would never allow their children to be friends with Davie again, and I was right. Before the summer was over, all Davies so-called friends stopped talking to him and when school started the bullying began. Davie began to hate going to school by his sophomore year, but he went anyway. It was right before the Christmas break Davie didn't come home after a night on the town. He said he was going to meet up with some of his old friends who wanted to apologize to him and become friends again. I had a bad feeling about that night, but he never told me who he was meeting with that night. So, when Davie never came home that night, or the next morning, I began calling all the friends I knew he had lost, but no one wanted to admit they were with Davie that night. So, I called the police to report him missing," June came clean with Brenda, and she could tell it had been eating her up inside for so many years. Brenda could tell June was relieving a ton of grief she felt for not being able to protect Davie from all the hate the town had to throw at him for being different.

Brenda let June express all her emotions as she told her story for the first time in years. Brenda knew there was nothing more she could do now, except to sit and listen to June. Allowing her to accept the pain and begin to grieve for her son, Davie. Brenda lost track of time sitting with June, to the point it was dark outside by the time Brenda received a call on the radio from the station.

"Detective Wisely, could you call the station?" the dispatcher announced over the radio.

Brenda took a moment to make sure June was going to be okay before she took out her phone to call the station. Once Brenda was satisfied June would be okay, she excused herself from the home and told June she would be in touch with her in the coming days, and if June needed anything to give her a call. Brenda gave June her personal cell number before leaving the house to begin her journey back to town. Brenda would make her call to the station while driving back to town.

Once Brenda was on the road back to Whispering Pine, she made the call into the station.

"This is Detective Wisely, is there something you need from me?" Brenda asked the dispatcher.

"Yes, Detective. There was a complaint about you today from a teacher at the high school. Sheriff Harper would like to know why you were at the school today speaking to teachers?"

"As Sheriff Harper is aware, I am reviewing the cold case of David Youngblood, and since his remains have now been found in a well on Mr. Browns land, I am reopening the case. Is there anything else the Sheriff needs to know?" Brenda did not hold back on her reply to the station's dispatcher.

"Yes, Sheriff Harper would like to meet with you tomorrow morning to go over what you may have uncovered during your investigation," the dispatcher related to Brenda before ending the call.

Brenda wanted to meet with the Sheriff as well. It was time she was told the truth about the first investigation and why no one followed up on Davie's case. She was able to find out more than the original investigation offers in one day, and what she had uncover so far should have been found by them as well, which was not noted in their initial reports.

After the call ended, Brenda continued her way towards her house, hoping Dalton was still up for dinner. She felt bad for not being home when Dalton got home from school, or even being there to cook dinner before it got too late, but she had a feeling Dalton would understand why she was late. She just needed to get home to tell him about her day, without giving away too much information. Not that she didn't trust Dalton, but she didn't want anyone to know more about her case than she did, being a small town and all.

Robert Starnes

Chapter 5

The Hunters Secret

Brenda decided she needed to ask her nosey neighbor, Joy, for some follow-up questions about the townspeople. She found it hard to believe that a child could have been murdered in such a small town, where everyone knew everything, but no one knew a thing about Davie's murder. Brenda felt she could get more gossip or rumors from Joy, even if she claimed she thought Davie moved away to be with relatives.

The next day, Brenda walked a few houses down from her home until she reached Joy's pathway to her front porch. She hoped going to Joy's home would make her feel more comfortable while gossiping about other residents of Whispering Pines. Brenda softly knocked on Joy's porch door until she saw Joy walking toward her from around the side of her home.

"Oh, Brenda, it's you. I'm so glad you decided to stop by. I was just thinking about you," Joy excitedly expressed to Brenda.

"Good morning, Joy. I thought I would come by this morning to chat a bit more since we were cut short the other day by my work call. I hope it is okay," Brenda politely addressed Joy.

"Yes, it is perfectly fine. You are welcome to stop by here anytime you want. What are neighbors for?" Joy spoke with glee as she walked up to her front door to open it and usher Brenda inside.

Brenda was startled as soon as she walked into Joy's home. Her home décor had a very country appeal, a little more than Brenda could take. As she followed Joy into the living room, she noticed a lot of ceramic plates lining the hall walls, all decorated with a chicken of some kind on them. Brenda was even more surprised to see the home décor spread into the living room. She wondered why country folk were so involved with anything with a chicken on it, but she didn't say anything to Joy about her taste in home décor. Joy left Brenda in the living room so she could go to the kitchen to get some iced tea for them.

As Joy returned to the living room, where Brenda was patiently waiting, with two glasses of sweet tea. Joy handed Brenda one glass and the other for herself. The two of them sat for a few moments in silence, so they could wet their whistle with the sweet tea. The sweetness of the tea was a bit more than Brenda could handle, so she stopped drinking her tea and set her glass on the coffee table and looked over toward Joy.

"Joy, do you mind if I ask you a few more questions about the case I am working on?"

"Of course not. I will do my best to answer your questions to the best of my knowledge," Joy joyfully replied to Brenda.

"Well, first, what can you tell me about the rumors of Davie going to live with relatives up north?" Brenda quickly began her questioning.

"You must understand that rumors in this town are like wildfires; they are quick to start but hard to put out. With that being said, I couldn't pinpoint who I heard it from, but it became factual after so many years. Everyone just assumed Davie left because it was all they were hearing then. No one suspects Davie is dead or will return one day. Why do you ask?" Joy suddenly questioned.

"Joy, I have some added information about Davie's disappearance. Now, what I am about to tell you must remain between us. We have not released any of the information to the public yet. Can you keep it quiet for now?" Brenda knew Joy could not keep the latest information quiet for too long. That was exactly what Brenda was hoping.

"You don't have to worry about me telling anyone anything. Your secret is safe with me. So, spill," Joy excitedly gestured for Brenda to continue.

"Thank you, Joy. We have confirmed some remains found the other day are, in fact, David

Youngblood. His skeletal remains were found at the bottom of a well in Klienstown on a residential property," Brenda began telling Joy some selected facts she wanted to get out to the residents of Whispering Pines.

"Let me guess, Henry Brown's land. Residents have always used his land for hunting or an occasional bonfire for the school students," Joy quickly revealed information Brenda had not been made aware of previously.

"Why would you assume Davie's remains were found on Mr. Brown's land? Just because people hunt there, and the school has bonfires for the students on the same land. Is there something you are not telling me why you would assume Mr. Brown's property?" Brenda wanted Joy to elaborate more on her answer.

"Well, like I said before, I don't get into gossip much here, but I heard more goes on out on his land than just hunting. Some people have said they had been to some, not so legal, dice games, and many times some high school students were there. But it's all just speculation, as I have never seen what I have just told you," Joy tried covering her tracks from her earlier statement.

"Thank you, Joy. I'm so sorry, but I must leave now. I didn't realize the time. I must get into the office before Sheriff Harper comes looking for me. Thank you for the tea. We will have to do this again sometime," Brenda expressed gratitude for the hospitality she received from Joy as she quickly exited her home.

Brenda walked home and got into her car. She now knew who she needed to speak to next. Brenda wanted to get firsthand knowledge of the rumors about Brown's land from the owner himself.

Brenda backed out of her driveway and turned her car to head to Main Street. She was ready for her fifteen-minute drive out to Klienstown to visit Mr. Brown. As Brenda left Whispering Pines, she noticed some of the locals watching her. It appeared Joy had quickly spread the information Brenda had shared with her through the grapevine, just as Brenda predicted. She drove down Country Club Road until she reached the highway. She knew she was only a few short minutes from her destination, Mr. Brown's place.

Brenda made a quick right off the highway and onto a county road that led to Henry Brown's home. When she arrived at his driveway, she slowed down, entering with caution. Brenda was aware many of the homeowners in Whispering Pines and surrounding areas protected their land with firearms. She did not want to start a war. Brenda was only there to have a conversation with Mr. Brown.

Brenda stopped her car a short way back from Mr. Brown's truck, so it didn't look like she was trying to block him in for any reason. After her car was in park, Brenda walked up to Mr. Brown's front door. She made it to his door without incident and was happy to see Mr. Brown was waiting for her.

"Good morning, Mr. Brown. I don't know if you remember me, but I am Detective Wisely. I was here the other day when you found the skeletal remains on your land. I was wondering if you had a moment for a few questions?" Brenda casually asked Mr. Brown.

"Please, call me Henry. Would you like to come in so we could talk?" Henry replied.

"Thank you. I will not take up too much of your time. These are just some follow-up questions. I'm sure you were expecting me," Brenda tried to get some confirmation he knew she had already spoken to Joy.

"No, I wasn't expecting you to come back, but since you are here, ask away," Henry indicated to Brenda.

"Great. First, I would like to ask how well you knew the victim?"

"Not very well. I believe Davie was one of my students at one time, but I can't be too sure," Henry replied to Brenda.

"Student? Were you a teacher at Whispering Pines? I did not see your name as one of Davie's teachers when I gathered his class schedules from Elementary or High School. What class did you teach, and what grade?" Brenda shockingly replied.

"Yes, I retired several years ago. I used to teach history in Junior High, sixth grade," Henry openly replied.

"That explains it, I did not get Davie's class schedules for Junior High. May I ask why you retired? You look too young to retire," Brenda quickly asked.

"I am much older than I may look. I am fifty-five and retired at forty-nine. There was an incident at one of the school events, and I may have been accused of something I didn't do. Since there was no proof, I was asked to retire early. It was the only way the school could save face with the residents of Whispering Pines. I am not allowed to elaborate any more on the subject, as all of us had to sign an NDA. You understand, don't you? Now, what other questions do you have for me?" Henry quickly shot past his discretions and forced Brenda's focus back on Davie.

"If you were asked to retire early by the school, why do you still provide land for the schools to use for events, such as bonfires?"

"I may have been asked to retire early, but I own much of the land here in Anderson County. Henry explained to Brenda that he wanted to ensure the students had safe and enjoyable activities supervised by parents and teachers," Henry explained to Brenda.

"It seems like you love the town and its people to be so kind after something not so pleasant happening with you and the school," Brenda complimented Henry.

"Well, I am glad we got those questions out of the way. I hope they help in your investigation. Now, if there is nothing more, I need to head out to one of my pastures to feed the cattle," Henry tried to end the questioning from Brenda, but she was not ready to end their talk.

"I'm not finished with you yet. I still have more questions. Did Davie ever attend any of these school events on your land?"

"I'm sure he did, but we did not have sign-up sheets for students who attended. The events were not mandatory, so if they wanted to come, they would. And if they didn't want to come, they didn't."

"Who do you think may have a record of who came to the events? I am not looking at all the events that may have happened on your land, but just the ones that may have occurred before December 2014, the month Davie went missing."

"You could ask his friends or maybe one of the teachers who chaperoned the events."

"Was it always the same teachers who chaperoned?"

"Pretty much. Some parents switched off and on with who would attend as well."

"Do you know what teachers went to all of them? Or maybe some of the parents who may have attended?"

"The only teachers I can recall attending all the events were Mr. Stillman, Mrs. Ingram, and Ms. Carter. I am not sure which parents went, but the teachers might remember."

"Now, besides the school events you allowed on your land, are there any other events that may have gone on out here that were not school-related?" Brenda began to switch her questions from student events to maybe some other types of illegal adult events.

"I am not sure what you are asking me. Are you asking if I may have had some types of parties here? I can assure you if there was a party here, it was legal."

"I'm going to ask you straight out. Did you have illegal dice or card games out on any of your properties at any time? Remember, I am not here to bust you on anything you may have done in the past unless it directly ties to Davie's murder," Brenda asked Henry to confirm what Joy had told her earlier.

Henry took a moment to think about Detective Wisely's question before answering. Brenda was not sure if Henry was trying hard to remember if there were such events that had gone on or if he was trying to think about how much he would tell her.

"Is there a problem, Henry?" Brenda pressed for an answer.

"No ma'am, there is no problem. I don't think that is a question I can answer without speaking to the Sheriff first. As you can appreciate, I know I have rights, and I do not have to answer your questions unless I am being detained or have a lawyer present. Am I under arrest and need to contact an attorney?" Henry quickly shut down Brenda's questions.

"No, sir. You are not under arrest yet. But if I find out you are hiding something from me about Davie's murder, I will be back with an arrest warrant, and our next conversation will be at the station with your attorney. Are you confident your answers do not have anything to do with Davie's murder?" Brenda threatened Mr. Brown.

"Again, Detective Wisely, I have nothing more to say. But if I think of anything else that may help you in your investigation, I will contact you," Mr. Brown concluded his conversation with Brenda and stood up to escort her out of his home.

Brenda stood up, followed Henry toward his front door, and exited his home. She did not look back at Mr. Brown as she walked to her car. She did not want Mr. Brown to see how angry she was about his refusal to answer her last question. After Brenda was inside her car, she buckled her seatbelt and backed out of his driveway. Brenda felt she did not get the answers she wanted from Mr. Brown. She was, however, able to get more information about some of the teachers she had already been in contact with. She felt it was time for her to go back and ask a few follow-up questions of those teachers.

Brenda decided to head straight to the high school because she wanted to speak to Mr. Stillman again. She sensed he was evasive during their first encounter and wanted to gather more information. Brenda radioed into the station to let them know where she was headed next, and that she would stop by the station after. The dispatcher informed her that Sheriff Harper wanted to speak to her when she was finished, so going to the station afterward was perfect.

Brenda ended the radio transmission and proceeded through town until she was sitting in the high school parking lot, for the second time. She parked her car and before returning to Mr. Stillman's classroom, not wanting to speak with Mrs. Cater first, in the administration office.

Brenda walks straight into the Administration Office she greeted Mrs. Carter first, this time.

"Mrs. Carter, do you have a place where you and I can speak for a few minutes?" Detective Wisely questioned before Mrs. Carter could greet her back.

"Hello, Detective Wisely, what is it that you would like to talk about?" Mrs. Carter responded kindly.

"It's about Davie's cold case, is there somewhere private we can talk?" Detective Wisely asked again.

"Yes, follow me, we can speak in the teachers' lounge since they are all in class," Mrs. Carter answered Detective Wisely while walking past her and into the hallway.

The two of them walk a short way down the hallway until Mrs. Carter stops at a door that read 'Teacher's Lounge.'

"Right through here, Detective," Mrs. Carter pushes open the door and holds it open for Brenda to go in first.

Brenda walks past Mrs. Carter into the lounge and takes a seat at the closest empty table. Once Brenda was seated, Mrs. Carter walks over to the table Brenda has chosen then takes a seat across from her. When they were both settled at the table, Mrs. Carter had something to say.

"Would you like a coffee, water, or soda before we begin?"

"No, thank you. I have come into some information about the regular chaperons who attended all the school events which took place out on Mr. Brown's land. You were named as one of three who chaperoned every event out there. Is there anything you can remember about the event that took place the night before Davie ran away?" Detective Wisely began her interview.

"I am not sure I understand what you are asking me. Are you asking me if I remember everything that happened at every event which took place there? There were so many events over the years I can remember all of them off the top of my head," Mrs. Carter replies to Detective Wisely's broad question.

"No, I am only asking you if you remember anything happening at the event the night before Davie ran away, as you claim. You would think a night before a beloved student goes missing would be a night ingrained in your mind. Again, did you see or hear anything that night?" Detective Wisely has taken off her gloves and is asking a specific question.

"There is not much I can tell you about that night because I was not there," Mrs. Carter told Detective Wisely.

"What do you mean, you were not there? Everyone I have spoken to said you and the two others were three people who attended every school event. Why were you not there that night?" Detective Wisely questioned Mrs. Carter.

"Look, what I am about to tell you cannot leave this room, because I will deny it if it does come out. My night could cost me my job, so can you tell me it is between us?" Mrs. Carter expands her thoughts to Brenda.

"I can promise you as long as it does not have anything to do with Davie's disappearance or the investigation, then it will be just between us," Detective Wisely promises a nervous Mrs. Carter.

"I was there, but I was not there. You see, the year Davie ran away, I was sleeping with one of my students and I was with him that night. We were both there that night, but we had walked away from the crowd to an empty old house on Mr. Browns land and were there the entire night. We only made it back to the event right before it ended so we could both be seen there and before you ask, I will tell you it was not Davie. I will not tell you the student's name because it ended that year,"

Mrs. Carter admits to Detective Wisely with an assumed look on her face.

Brenda took in what Mrs. Carter told her and replied, "As long as the student you were with that night does not become a suspect in Davie's disappearance, I will not ask you his name and this will stay between us. I will let you know that if you ever sleep with a student again and I hear about it, I will be back here to take you in, and your past will become known. Do you understand what I am telling you?" Detective Wisely boldly threatened Mrs. Carter.

"Yes, I understand, and I can assure you it has never happened since then and never will again," Mrs. Carter acknowledged the detective's threats.

Brenda ended her interview with Mrs. Carter, left the teacher's lounge and began to make her way down the halls one more time until she got to Mr. Stillman's classroom door. He was the next teacher she wanted to re-interview since her last conversation.

As Brenda stepped up to Mr. Stillman's classroom door, she peeped in through the window in the door. She noticed his class was full of students. To her surprise, Dalton was in the class. Brenda was not prepared to interrupt Mr. Stillman's class, especially with her son in the class, so she decided to wait at the end of the hallway. She waited until the class bell rang and the students exited Mr. Stillman's class before she walked back to his room. Brenda wanted to avoid being seen by Dalton or any of his friends. She didn't want him to be embarrassed that she was there.

Brenda walked through Mr. Stillman's open classroom door and quietly shut the door behind her. She didn't want anyone to hear the questions she was about to ask.

Mr. Stillman looked up with a sense of shock on his face. It was obvious he was not expecting to see Detective Wisely back in his room any time soon after their last encounter.

"Detective Wisely, what can I do for you today?" Mr. Stillman questioned the Detective's appearance in his room.

"Mr. Stillman, it has been brought to my attention that you and a few other teachers chaperone school events that happened on Mr. Brown's land. Is that correct?" Brenda went straight for the tough questions.

Mr. Stillman didn't answer as quickly as he had before, but he knew the events would be eventually found out. So, he felt it was time to tell her everything he knew about Mr. Brown's land.

"Yes, Detective, you are correct. Mr. Brown allows the school to use his land for dedicated events such as a homecoming bonfire. The school has been using his land for many years. The events are supposed to provide a safe place for students to have an enjoyable time and stay out of trouble. Not only are some teachers at the events chaperoning, but several of the students' parents also take turns supervising the students. What do the events on Mr. Brown's land have to do with your investigation?" Mr. Stillman asked in return.

"With the teachers and parents being at these events, then if anything happened to a student, someone would know about it, correct? I mean, you are there to prevent things from happening to anyone. As you said, you were providing a safe place for students to keep them out of trouble," Brenda avoided his question and continued with her line of questions.

"That is correct. But you must understand there could be some incidents that happen that we may not see or even know about. Kids are crafty to avoid always being watched at an event," Mr. Stillman replied.

"What types of incidents?" Brenda questioned, in an attempt, to get more from Mr. Stillman.

"You know, sometimes a student or two may have brought alcohol to an event, which we may not have known about until after. We have heard some students were being bullied at the events, but we never saw it happen, and we were not informed about those incidents until after the fact," Mr. Stillman did not like the way the Detective's questions were going.

"So, if a student happened to get hurt at an event you didn't see or weren't told about until later, what would happen to the students who started the incident?" Brenda pressed on.

"It would depend on what the incident was. There have been times when some students have received detention for their actions. But there have never been any serious incidents to happen at a school event," Mr. Stillman quickly added.

"How can you be sure a serious incident hasn't happened? What if an incident happened at an event, but no one ever discussed it after the fact?" Brenda was trying to draw a line in the sand.

"We would know. Nothing ever happens in this town without everyone knowing about it a day after it happens," Mr. Stillman wanted to assure Detective Wisely everyone knew everything.

"I see. What other events happened at Mr. Brown's, you know, the adult events," Brenda decided to change her tactic to get more information about more serious adult parties Mr. Brown may have had on his land.

"I am unaware of any other types of events Mr. Brown may have had on his land. You will need to speak to him if you want to know how he spends his weekends," Mr. Stillman didn't divulge any more for Detective Wisely to go on.

"Thank you, Mr. Stillman. I know you have class soon, so I will leave for the time being. If I have any more questions for you, I will have them down at the station," Brenda expressed to Mr. Stillman as she stood up and began walking toward the classroom door. She knew it was time for her to go speak with Sheriff Harper.

Robert Starnes

Chapter 6

Christopher's Guilt

Brenda made her way to the station to have a meeting with Sheriff Harper about her questioning of Mr. Brown. While she knew she was doing her job, she was still curious as to what Sheriff Harper had to say about it. Brenda parked in front of the station and made her way inside and to her surprise Sheriff Harper was waiting for her, who quickly waved for her to follow him into his office.

Brenda followed Sheriff Harper's suggestion and followed him into his office and shut the door behind her. After the door was closed, she walked up and stood in front of Sheriff Harper's desk as he sat in his chair looking up at her. After a moment, he asked Brenda to have a seat.

Brenda took a seat in one of the old chairs in the office and waited for Sheriff Harper to begin.

"Detective, I heard, you went out to Mr. Brown's property and questioned him. May I ask what led you back to him?" Sheriff Harper casually asked Brenda.

"Well, not only was the victims' remains found on his property, but I was informed that many class events are held out on his properties. Those two things gave me probable cause to question him, do you not agree?" Brenda shot back at the Sheriff.

"Yes, I agree with you, but you must understand, we are a small town and if we go around accusing people, or even suggesting, of committing murder, their lives would be ruined just because of the allegation. We do police work a little differently here, as you may have noticed. We only question people if we have more than just probable cause, we like hard evidence," Sheriff Harper replied.

"So, the appearance of someone's guilt is more important than finding out the truth? How are we supposed to get hard evidence if we are not allowed to question people?" Brenda inquired. "Doesn't the victim, or their family, have rights as well? Shouldn't we be questioning everyone to gather information about what could have happened so we can narrow down our focus to finding the actual murderer?"

"Those are all valid points, Detective, but this is not a big city you are used to working in. Interviewing the wrong person could also impede your investigation. If you interview the wrong person, they could relay information to who may have committed the crime and may even help them cover up the crime. These people have known each other since childhood, and why they may think they are just 'helping' a friend out, inadvertently becoming an accessory after the fact. We don't want to create more offenders if we can help it," Sheriff Harper elaborated a bit more on small town investigations.

Brenda sat back in her seat, taking in what Sheriff Harper had just explained to her about small town investigations. While she was not keen on the idea of interviewing people, she understood where Sheriff Harper came from.

"I understand, now, Sheriff Harper. I can see how interviewing people could damage the investigation. I am not here to accuse everyone of murder. Right now, I just want to find justice for Davie Youngblood and his poor grieving mother. I will try to be a bit more casual with my questions moving forward. Now, is it all right if I speak to Davie's best friend, Christopher Wooden? I just want to talk to him about his friendship with Davie, before high school," Brenda asked the Sheriff.

"You may speak to Christopher, but remember, you are not interviewing him, you are just talking to him," Sheriff Harper expressed to Brenda to use some restraint with her questions.

"Yes, sir, and thank you," Brenda concluded her meeting with Sheriff Harper, stood up and walked out of his office.

Brenda continued straight out of the station to her car and drove away. Her only thought while she was driving back to the high school was how she was going to approach Christopher. She did not want to be too aggressive with him, so she could get information from him, but she also didn't want to be seen as a pushover.

As Brenda approached the high school, once again, she parked her vehicle on the side of the school. Again, she did not want to draw attention to herself, or cause drama for her son, Dalton.

Noticing the time, Brenda knew school would be letting out in just over an hour, she wanted to make sure Mr. Wooden had time to speak to her at the school. She needed to find out if Mr. Wooden had a free class period at the time of her arrival, so she decided she needed to stop back into the Administration Office and speak to Ms. Carter about Mr. Woodens' class schedule. As soon as Brenda walked into the office she was quickly greeted by Ms. Carter.

"Hello, Detective Wisely, what can I do for you today?" Ms. Carter loudly spoke out to Brenda.

"Hello Ms. Carter, I would like to know if Mr. Wooden has a free class this period? I would like to speak to him for a moment, if possible," Brenda replied to Ms. Carter.

"Let me check," Ms. Carter responded casually to Detective Wisely.

After a moment of looking up Mr. Woodens' class schedule on a computer, she returned to Detective Wisely.

"Yes, it seems Mr. Wooden is free right now. His classroom is room 119, just down the West hallway. Is there anything else I may assist you with?" Ms. Carter asked Detective Wisely.

"No, I have all I need right now but thank you for your assistance," Brenda ended her conversation with Ms. Carter and walked out of the Administration office.

Brenda took a sharp right as she exited the office and proceeded to make her way down the West hallway until she reached room 119. As she approached the door, she noticed Mr. Wooden had another teacher in his classroom. They seemed to be in a serious conversation, but Brenda went ahead and knocked on the closed door.

When Brenda knocked on the door, both Mr. Wooden and the other teacher looked in her direction, and the unknown teacher quickly stood up and proceeded to walk over to the door.

The door was suddenly opened by the other teacher who was quickly leaving, which Brenda wanted to ask as to why he was leaving so fast, but she knew she had to play it cool. She decided she would circle back to find out who the teacher was and why they left so quickly, but she was only there to talk with Mr. Wooden.

Brenda excused herself for the passing teacher and slowly walked into Mr. Woodens classroom. As she entered the room, she quietly asked if the person in the room was Mr. Wooden.

He quickly responded yes and asked her to come in and take a seat. Once she was seated, she reached into her breast pocket of her shirt and pulled out a small notebook and pen, as Mr. Wooden looked at her with wonder.

"Hello, Mr. Wooden. I am Detective Wisely, and I am new here in Whispering Pines. I was wondering if we could talk about an old friend of yours," Brenda began a casual dialog with Mr. Wooden. "Do you mind if I call you Christopher?"

"Chris is fine, actually, and what can I do for you Detective?" Chris corrected Brenda.

"Sorry, Chris. Do you remember an old friend of yours named David Youngblood?"

"Yes, Detective, I remember Davie. What would you like to know?"

"I was just wondering, how long were you and Davie friends?"

"I had known Davie since Kindergarten, up until he disappeared. But we were only friends until eighth grade, why do you ask?"

"I am working on Davie's cold case and ran across a report in his file. The report was a statement you made during the first investigation. If I remember correctly, you said you and Davie were not friends at all and you had no information on Davie's disappearance, but in another report, I found, one of your classmates insisted in their statement you were in fact best friends. My question is, why would you claim not to have been friends with Davie at the time?"

"I don't remember exactly what I said back then, but it must have been a misunderstanding, or a misprint in the report. I never said we were never friends, but I did say I didn't have any information on his disappearance," Chris clarified with Detective Wisely.

"Forgive me, you are correct. The report had a note on it saying it was incorrect. Thank you for clarifying for me. May I ask, what changed in your relationship, in the eighth grade, to make you not be friends anymore?" Brenda hoped her question did not make Chris shut down so early in her questioning.

"Nothing really happened between us, we just grew apart. Our interests changed the summer after eighth grade. I became more interested in sports, like football, basketball, and baseball, while his interests were more about being in the high school band. It wasn't anything major, we both changed, I guess," Chris openly and honestly answered Detective Wisely's question.

"Thank you for your honesty, Chris, but I believe I read in one of your classmates' reports, you told them Davie changed during the summer and you could not be friends with him anymore. Why would one of your classmates say something like that? What do you think they meant by 'changed?' In their report, it sounded serious, or why else would they tell the officer questioning them about the change?" Brenda felt she could dig a little deeper without causing Chris to end their conversation.

"I am not one to get into rumors, but I know there was a rumor Davie came out during the summer in question. I can assure you that is not the reason we stopped being friends. I would not have cared if Davie was gay or not, he was my best friend for so many years, it would not have made a difference. I can tell, not only did many of our classmates have a problem with the rumor, but so did many of the parents," Chris explained to Detective Wisely.

"Since you brought it up, how exactly did the other students and parents feel about the rumor?"

"All I can tell you is after the rumor began spreading around town, many parents of our classmates demanded their children to stop being friends with Davie. The parents felt it was best for their children to not be associated with a gay person, so everyone stopped being his friend. I knew Davie was having a tough time with how things were being dealt with over just a rumor and I did nothing about it. I feel horrible for not staying friends, but I moved away after the first day of our freshman year. I did not return to Whispering Pines until the middle of our sophomore year and by that time, Davie and I did not have a chance to become friends again, because he disappeared just a month after my return. I feel so much guilt for not being there for Davie when he needed a friend the most. I heard many of our classmates gave Davie hell for the entire year," Chris expressed sympathy for Davie as he spoke, Brenda could see it in his eyes and the tone of his voice.

Hearing what Davie went through at the beginning of high school saddened Brenda deeply. She never understood how parents could teach their children such bad manners they would alienate another student based on a rumor.

"You wouldn't know the names of some of those parents, would you? Or maybe the classmates who may have treated Davie the worst, would you?"

"It's no secret here in Whispering Pines who the students were and who their parents are. Many of my classmates still live here in Whispering Pines and hold high positions in the City Counsel. Others are well respected here as well because they own the dairy farm and ranches here. Many of them are big supporters of our city fundraisers, so speaking to them will not be easy. If you can get a conversation in with one of them, it would only be a few hours before everyone you wanted to speak to knew you would be coming and find ways to avoid speaking to you. So, if I was you, I would tread lightly and make sure you select the right person to start with, or find another way to get to them," Chris gave Brenda some advice.

Brenda felt Chris was being sincere with his advice and figured he knew what he was talking about.

"Chris, does the school have any upcoming events scheduled? Maybe one which would require parents to attend?"

"Actually, I have something better for you. Our five-year class reunion is coming up in a few weeks. Everyone you would want to speak to will be there," Chris offered an idea for the Detective.

"Really? How can you be sure everyone will be attending?" Brenda questioned Chris.

"We are a small town with small graduation classes. We only had forty-two graduates when I graduated. Most of them still live here, like I mentioned before, and the others do not live far away. Every one of my classmates will be there, rest assured," Chris happily responded to Brenda.

"Interesting. It sounds like your class reunion is exactly the type of event I need. Thank you for letting me know. Can I ask you not to tell anyone about our conversation today? If not for me, keep it between us for Davie. I am only trying to find out who murdered him," Brenda responded without thinking.

"Excuse me? Did you say Davie's murder?" Chris quickly questioned.

"I'm so sorry to have to tell you this, but Davie's remains were discovered a few days ago. He was found in a well on the outskirts of town. It has been decided Davie never ran away, or just vanished, but was murdered and thrown down the well," Brenda expressed her deepest apologies to Chris.

"You mean to tell me Davie never left the town? Someone from here murdered him and just threw his body down a well like trash," Chris took a moment to compose himself before speaking again. "Let me guess, the well was one of those out on Mr. Brown's land?" Chris quickly said aloud to Brenda's surprise.

"Why would you suspect his remains were found on Mr. Brown's land? Do you know something you have not informed me about?" Detective Wisely rapidly responded.

"No, it's just that many of the school events held out on Mr. Brown's land got wild at times when I was in school. Students would beat up other kids and were drunk at most of the events. The events now are not much different to be honest," Chris explained his comment.

"Are the teachers who chaperon, or the parents who attend, informed about those types of activities during the events?" Brenda needed some clarification to the accusation.

"Of course, they know about those things happening, but they do nothing about it because most of the students involved these days parents are the ones who took part in those activities when we were in school. The teachers who chaperon know as well, most of those things happen right in front of them, but they don't do anything to keep the parents friendly with them," Chris finished.

"I see. Did any of those beating happen to Davie when you were in school?" Brenda needed to find out a bit more before she moved on.

"I can't be too sure about high school, since I was gone after the first day of freshman year, but I do know he was beat up at some of those events when we were in middle school."

"Thank you for letting me know. I promise you I will do everything in my power to get justice for Davie. It sounds like you miss him," Detective Wisely concluded her interview with Chris.

Before Brenda walked out of the classroom, Chris said something as she was leaving.

"I do miss him. He was my best friend and now I wish I had stayed in town or stayed in touch with Davie. Maybe things would have turned out differently for him."

"Don't put thoughts like those into your head. There was nothing you could have done to prevent Davies murder. It was done in a fashion to suggest a large cover-up. With the information you gave me, I now have other leads I can follow up on, so thank you, Chris."

Chris's face showed how much guilt he was feeling for abandoning his best friend back then and finding out he was murdered made it worse for him. Brenda felt pity for Chris as she turned and walked out of his classroom.

Brenda managed to leave the high school without Dalton, or other students seeing her there. As she walked back to her car, she couldn't shake the feeling there was so much more about those school events out on Mr. Brown's land and she was determined to figure out what else could have happened out there. She knew who her next meeting needed to be with tomorrow, but she needed to make sure it was okay with Sheriff Harper.

Brenda chose to drive by the station to see if Sheriff Harper was still in so she could ask him about her next interviewee. While she was pulling up to the station, she noticed the Sheriff's car was still parked in the same spot as it was when she saw him that morning.

Brenda parked and walked into the station, passing the dispatcher walking straight to Sheriff Harpers office. When she arrived at his door, she noticed he was speaking to someone she had not seen before. She was not sure if she should interrupt them or wait for their meeting to be down with. Brenda decided to wait until the morning to speak to the Sheriff, so she decided to continue home and wait for Dalton to get in from school. She thought it was a good night for her to cook dinner and have time to catch-up with Dalton about school.

Brenda arrived at her house and noticed Dalton had not made it in yet, so she went inside to start preparing dinner to surprise Dalton.

When Dalton got home, he was surprised at the home-cooked meal waiting for him but sat down at the table. Once he was seated Brenda began catching up with her only son and she loved every minute of their time together.

Chapter 7

The Sheriff's Confession

The next morning, Brenda got up and ready a little earlier than usual because she wanted to make sure she met with Sheriff Harper as soon as he came in. She was ready to plead her case with the Sheriff for his approval for the next person she wanted to speak to. It was going to be a hard sell for her because the person she wanted to speak to was the earlier Sheriff of Whispering Pines. The same Sheriff who was in charge when Davie went missing. She needed answers he could possibly provide.

Brenda walked into the station and looked to see if the Sheriff had made it in yet and to her surprise, he was already at his desk. Once she saw him in his office, she quickly walked over to his door and knocked, even though it was already open.

Hearing the knock on his door, the Sheriff looked up from his desk and saw Brenda standing there. He began to wonder what she was up to for the day.

"Detective Wisely, what a surprise to see you here this early. What can I do for you?" Sheriff Harper immediately questioned.

"I was wondering if I could run something by you, if you have a moment," Brenda quietly asked the Sheriff.

"Sure, what's on your mind?"

"I was wondering if it would be possible for me to speak to the previous Sheriff. Does Wyatt Dawson still live in Whispering Pines?"

"He sure does. Now, why would you want to speak to him? He has not been on the job in many years. I doubt there is any insight he can provide for you for your investigation," Sheriff Harper replied.

"There have been some concerns of events which may have taken place when he was Sheriff on Mr. Brown's land. I wanted to see if I could get some more insight into what he may know or may have heard back then."

Sheriff Harper took a moment to understand what Brenda had just asked him. He knew it would be tricky for her to interview Wyatt, being he left on bad terms for the station when he was not re-elected for Sheriff. After thinking about how Wyatt would take Brenda's questions, he made his decision.

"I don't see why not. I'm sure he would jump at an opportunity to relive his glory days as the Sheriff. Just don't try to press him too hard," Sheriff Harper approved Brenda's request.

Brenda thanked the Sheriff and took off out of the station so fast, the dispatcher asked the Sheriff if there was an emergency she was not aware of. Sheriff Harper quickly told the dispatcher who Brenda was going to interview, and she looked at the Sheriff as if he was joking. Seeing he was not joking, the dispatcher slowly turned back to her station and said no more.

Brenda made a beeline for her car and quickly set her destination to Mr. Dawson's address. It was not hard to find his house since he lived off Main Street in town. His house still had old bootleg signs in his front yard from when he was running for another term as Sheriff. Apparently, it was too much for his loss to remove the signs and no one ever said anything to him about it.

Brenda pulled up and parked in his driveway right behind his old police car. She exited her car and went ahead to his front door.

Arriving at the front door she could tell the house had been long lived in. The paint was peeling off the exterior walls and front door. The place needed some upkeep for sure. She let her opinions of his house slowly slip into the back of her mind as she started knocking.

It only took Wyatt a minute to answer the door. As he opened his front door, he looked surprised to see a female at his door so early in the morning.

"What can I do for you this morning, ma'am?" Walton flirtatiously asked Brenda.

"Well, first you can address me as Detective Wisely. I am the new detective here in Whispering Pines and I am investigating a cold case from ten years ago. I thought I would stop by and see if you had any more to add to the reports, since you were Sheriff at the time," Brenda set Wyatt straight.

"Excuse me, Detective Wisely. What do you possibly think I could know about the case after ten years? I can't remember what day of the week it is most of the time. What makes this case special?" Wyatt proceeded to antagonize Brenda.

"I'm glad you asked. The cold case I began working on has become a murder investigation, now that his remains have being discovered," Brenda shot back at Wyatt.

Hearing how a cold case had turned into a murder investigation peaked Wyatt's interest.

"Which cold case are you referring to, if you don't mind me asking?"

"The case of David Youngblood. Does the name ring any bells?"

The look on Wyatt's face went from a look of having fun at Brenda's expense to a look of horror. Brenda didn't expect his reaction to change so drastically.

"Really? What gives you the idea his disappearance is nothing more than that? Why do you suspect he was murdered, Detective?"

"Because his skeletal remains were found a few days ago in a well on Mr. Brown's land. You know Henry Brown, don't you? He used to be a schoolteacher back in the day," Brenda questioned Wyatt's knowledge of the town's folk, being he was the Sheriff when Davie went missing.

"I have to say I am shocked to hear he was murdered. I thought for sure he just ran away. There were so many rumors going around about him being a fag. I assumed he couldn't take the torture he received at school every day and took off out of town," Wyatt told Brenda with no filter at all.

"Excuse me? Why do you feel it's okay to call a child such a word like that? Do you not respect the people you were elected to serve and protect?" Brenda said without thinking first, letting her emotions take over the questioning.

"You know what I mean, Detective. People were not so sensitive about words like that back then. Times are changing, but the people of Whispering Pines aren't. I am sorry if I offended you. Do you have a gay child as well?" Wyatt tried to explain his earlier comment with no luck.

"Excuse me? First, that is none of your business, but as far as I know, my son is not gay. But I would love him just as much if he was. I am not here to discuss my home-life, I am here to find out who killed Davie and why," Brenda let her emotions take over her mouth again. She was afraid she may have inadvertently told Wyatt she didn't know her son's sexuality and he may have thought the same thing. She was not prepared to have her son outed and not even because he was gay, but because of her mouth.

"Let's get back on topic if you don't mind. I am here to find out if you were aware of any incidents which may have happened on Mr. Browns land during any earlier school events back then?" Brenda tried to bring the subject back to the reason she was at his home in the first place.

"What do you want me to say, Detective? That I knew kids bullied other kids during those events. Well, yes. There may have been a few complaints from some parents about their children being bullied, or even beat up, at some of the school events out there. What about it? Kids are kids. If they don't like someone, there is nothing we can do to prevent them from beating up another kid. It's just how kids were back then and I'm sure they are the same today," Wyatt replied with no shame in his tone.

"You don't think a child going missing after one of those events on Mr. Brown's land seems suspicious? Then ten years later his remains are found on the same land as the school events were. Why didn't you press harder on the teacher and parents who were at those events? Were you scared you would lose the election, because it looks like you lost anyway," Brenda decided to take a stab at his pride.

"You don't know what you are talking about lady. I did everything I could to find out what happened to Davie, but to be honest, my hands were tied."

"And why were your hands tied during a missing child investigation? What could have been more important than finding out the truth about Davie," Brenda pleaded for Wyatt to answer honestly.

"Because I was aware of some illegal activities going on at an old house on Mr. Brown's land but looked the other way. It is not what you may be thinking I might add," Wyatt quickly responded.

"And what type of illegal activities went on at the house?"

"It was nothing really. Just some dice games and maybe some underage drinking. It was just a place where some adults and their children could have a fun time. You know, fathers teaching their son's how to be a man and since their parents were in attendance, I saw no need to bust the dice games. It's not like they were filming child porn, or anything like that, out there or trading children. It was just a regular dice game," so I looked the other way. That was until one of the minors had a car wreck in town after one of those games and I was going to arrest him but was threatened by his parents. He said if I went ahead with the arrest, he would inform the state I knew about the dice games and let them happen anyway. I would not have only lost my job, but I could have been arrested myself and I was not prepared to do time for allowing such an insignificant gambling event to happen, so I let the kid off," Wyatt came clean with Brenda.

"That's it? You just let a kid get away with drunk driving? There must be more to the story than that," Brenda pressed Wyatt harder.

"Fine, he hit a woman walking across the street. She was hurt and had to go to the hospital, but the woman hit by the son was reasonably compensated for her discretion and not pressing charges," Wyatt elaborated more on the actual incident.

Brenda took some time to soak in what Wyatt had just told her. First, she could not believe something so serious could be covered up so easily. A parent blackmailing the Sheriff and paying off a victim to keep their child from getting an arrest on his record.

"What else can you tell me about the parents of this town when Davie was in school and being tormented every day?"

"Let's just say if a poor parent called the station and tried to report a rich kid of bullying or assuring their child, those reports never went any further than the original complaint. You must understand a small town to know what I'm telling you. There are some families here in Whispering Pines who keep the town going. They are the richest families in town and have been for many years. So, if those rich families were ever implicated in anything illegal, or damaging to their image, it was swept under the rug. Everyone in town knows we must keep the rich families happy, or the town would die out."

"Is that so? Tell me, were any reports called in by Mrs. Youngblood about Davie back then?"

"I hate to say it, but yes. We received many calls from June after Davies eighth grade summer, just as he was beginning his freshman year, but nothing ever came of her calls," Wyatt seemed to be expressing sympathy for his actions back then.

"And who were the calls about? Which student or parent did she call about?"

"That's the saddest part. Most of her calls were about Davies' best friend, Chris Wooden. She would report Chris assaulted Davie on many occasions, and she was afraid for her son, but I couldn't do anything about it because Chris's father was the president of the bank.

Anyone who knew anything knew you didn't piss off the back president. Not if you expected to have a loan approved, or if you wanted your land to be repossessed by the bank. That is how much power he had and still has to this day," Wyatt told Brenda with certainty.

"You mean to tell me Davies' best friend, Christopher Wooden, was his biggest bully and abuser?"

"Yes, his mother reported it as so, but we never questioned the validity of her statements at the time. You know why we didn't, now anyway."

"Thank you, Mr. Dawson. I appreciate what you have told me today and I will do my best to keep the information you gave me today between us. I am beginning to understand how small towns work and I am not here to bring any undo resent from anyone to your door," Detective Wisely expressed to Mr. Dawson.

Before Brenda walked out of Wyatt's house, he had something to say to her.

"Detective, I am sorry I didn't investigate Davies' disappearance more than I did, but again, my hands were tied once certain people's name began coming up," Wyatt told Brenda with such a sad tone, she couldn't do anything but feel bad for Mr. Dawson. It sounded to Brenda that small town politics went deeper than she knew, but she was beginning to understand them. People with money in a small town seem to have more power than the police or any other town representative, and that did not sit well with her. In her eyes, no one was above the law, especially a murderer.

She began to believe she was going to make enemies of some of the rich town folk, but she was not worried about ruining her reputation, she wanted justice for a murdered child, even if it was over ten years ago. She was more determined to find out the truth more than ever. She was thrilled to know the class reunion was coming up soon and she would be able to get more gossip from Davies' earlier classmates, even if Chris wasn't expecting them to turn on him, she would soon find out if they would help him or turn. Based on what she already knew about a small town, it really didn't take much for one rumor to turn people against each other, so she just needed to wait a couple of weeks before she could get the truth.

Robert Starnes

Chapter 8

The Class Reunion

It had been two weeks since Brenda spoke to Wyatt and learned some truths about Davies' classmates and their parents. Brenda still could not understand how parents could defend their children who did such horrible things like covering up a child drinking and driving, hitting someone, then their parents blackmail the Sheriff and even pay off the victim in the drunk driving incident. All those things happened in Whispering Pines only because of how rich the parents were. Brenda was disgusted thinking about the privileges of the rich in Whisper Pines. Then hearing the one person who was supposedly Davies best friend was his biggest tormentor.

Brenda was up earlier than usual because she wanted to make sure she had everything she needed for her undercover questioning of Davies fellow students at their class reunion which was taking place that evening. She checked her recording equipment, making sure the batteries were all charged up and the microphones were working properly. Brenda wanted to make sure she could record each conversation so she could use those recordings later to write up her reports and findings. She did not want to take a notepad and pen with her because she felt people would talk more freely if they didn't know she was taking notes. Once Brenda checked everything and it was all working, she wanted to go shopping for an outfit to make sure she fit in at the reunion.

After Brenda finished shopping and getting her hair and nails done, we made it back home just in time to make dinner for Dalton. When they were finished eating, Brenda told Dalton she was going out for a few hours and would try to be home before ten o'clock. Dalton joked with her and told her not to do anything he wouldn't do, but to try to have fun. Brenda loved how she and Dalton could depend on each other and find a way to support each other. Setting the jokes aside, Brenda made her exit and headed to the school auditorium, where the class reunion was being held.

Brenda arrived at the reunion a few minutes early and decided to make her way inside to scope out the venue. She had never been to the school auditorium before and needed to see where she could set up shop for her discreet interviews. Brenda wanted to make sure where she conducted the interviews was a somewhat secluded area, not too close to the loudspeakers placed around the room. She also wanted to make sure there was enough lighting so she would watch the facial expressions of each interviewee. Everyone gives away details in their answers in their behavioral traits, like avoiding eye contact, leaving out minute details, repeating the questions, grooming behaviors, and sweating can all point to someone telling a lie. Brenda wanted to make sure she had plenty of lighting so she could detect those behaviors as she questioned each person.

With Brenda spot chosen, she noticed some of the guests had arrived and were making their way over to the check in table sitting near the entrance. Brenda made her way over to the table so she could get a look at each of her potential interviewees and match faces with names. She already had a preselected list of classmates she wanted to interview and by watching the guest's pickup their name tags gave her the faces to go with her list. Brenda sat near the check-in table until everyone arrived and picked up their name tags, then she decided to stroll around the room, listening to some of the casual conversation being had between old friends. From what she could gather, several of the guests were talking about Davie's remains being discovered and how heartbroken they were. She didn't overhear anyone confessing to his murder like she hoped, but she knew it wouldn't be easy for her to get what she came for. More in-depth background history of Davie and his bullies.

Thirty minutes later Brenda decided it was time for her to begin her interviews. Brenda took out the list of guests she wanted to speak with and first on the list was Max Sheppard. Max was one of Christopher's closest friends in school but did not keep in touch after school and she wanted to know why they didn't stay friends after graduating high school. Brenda walked up to Max and quietly asked if he could join her back at her preselected spot to speak to her. Max accepted the invitation and followed Brenda to the spot.

"Max, I am Detective Wisely, and I am investigating the disappearance of David Youngblood. Do you remember Davie?" Brenda began with a non-threatening question.

"Yes, Detective, I remember Davie. It was an extremely challenging time for us when he disappeared. Has something new come up? Is that the reason you are here?" Max seemed genuinely interested in the reason she was there.

"Yes. I am sorry to tell you, but Davie didn't disappear, he was murdered, and I am here to find out who killed him. And why they killed him. Can you help me with this?" Brenda wanted to make sure Max didn't feel like a suspect, but more like he could help her investigation.

Max took a moment to think about what Detective Wisely had just told him before answering.

"Yes, I will answer any question you have about Davie. Anything I can do to help. I will try to do my best. Davie may have been different from the other students, but he didn't deserve to be murdered. Do you have any suspects yet?"

"Thank you Max and I have no suspects currently. That is why I need your help. I need to find out more about how Davie was treated in school the summer before he started high school. Do you know who the students were, the ones who bullied Davie?"

"I am not one to speak ill of anyone, but it saddens me to tell you, but Davies' best friend, Chris, was the hardest on him. I knew Chris bullied Davie the entire summer, but at the time I didn't know why. They used to be such close friends then suddenly, Chris just began calling Davie names and started spreading rumors about him to everyone who would listen. And in this town even when someone wasn't listening, they still were. The worst part of it was even though most of our classmates didn't believe the rumors, everyone just started treating him badly. Looking back now, I wish I would have helped Davie, but I too was someone who treated him poorly. I have felt terrible about how I treated him ever since he was reported missing," Max began telling Brenda what she pretty much already knew. She wanted a bit more from Max.

"What kind of names did Chris call Davie and what were the rumors he started?" Brenda started to pry a little deeper into Max's recollection of events.

"Chris started telling everyone Davie was gay and tried to kiss him one night during the beginning of that summer. Next thing I know, everyone, including myself, began calling Davie a faggot, or queer. We never even gave Davie the chance to explain if it was even true. We all just jumped on the bandwagon and began treating Davie like crap. It was the lowest part of my life. Since then, I have tried to be a better person than I was back then," Max expressed to Brenda.

"You and Max were good friends when you graduated from high school but from what I have heard, you didn't keep in touch after school. Is there a reason you moved on without staying friends with Chris?" Brenda began asking the harder questions.

"Yes, we were friends in high school when he came back. He moved away for a year and returned right before Davie disappeared, sorry I mean murdered. Chris was not that popular in elementary school or middle school, but somehow when he came back to Whispering Pines, he seemed to be the most popular kid in school. I don't know why, but it's the truth. Maybe it was because his dad was, and still is, the president of the bank. Because of his status when he came back, of course, we became friends," Max elaborated on the social status change with Chris to Detective Wisely.

"Okay, I understand why you were friends. Now I want to know why you didn't remain friends?"

"Even though Chris and I were friends, we didn't always like doing the same things. We were both on the football team, but that was really about all we had in common. We were only friends in school, not really after school. While I would go home after school to work on our farm, Chris was more interested in partying and drinking. That was not really my scene."

"So, what you are telling me is Chris is not how he portrays himself to be? Not now or then?

"Correct. He is not the proper schoolteacher he wants everyone to think he is. He has a bad side," Max told Detective Wisely, hoping the questioning would soon be over because he didn't want to spend his evening thinking about his own horrible behavior in the past.

"Thank you, Max. Is there anything else you can tell me about Chris?"

"Not really but if you really want to know more about Chris, talk to Sarah. She was Chris's girlfriend throughout high school. If anyone knows more about

Chris it would be her," Max quickly gave Detective Wisely someone else to question.

"Thank you, Max. That is all I have for you this evening. Enjoy your night," Brenda ended her interview with Max. She was now ready to speak to Sarah, who was already on her list of people to talk to.

Brenda got up from the table she was sitting at talking with Max and found her way around the room to find Sarah. She didn't have to look extremely hard because Sarah seemed to be the center of attention at the reunion. It seems Sarah went on to make a name for herself by starting up a successful marketing firm in Dallas, TX. It was as if everyone wanted some reason to talk to Sarah, which included Brenda.

Brenda walked up to Sarah's circle and asked if she could speak to Sarah, alone. At first, Sarah didn't seem to be too thrilled about the prospect of leaving her circle of admirers, but she could tell by the look on Brenda's face it was not just a request.

Once they were back at Brenda's table, she began questioning Sarah.

"Sarah, I am Detective Wisely. I would like to ask you a few questions about an investigation I am conducting. Do you mind speaking with me?" Detective Wisely began the same way with Sarah as she did with Max. Just a simple question to get things going.

"It looks to me like I don't really have a choice, so what can I do for you?" Sarah sounded annoyed having to talk to anyone who was not a fan of hers.

"To be truthful, Sarah, you do have a choice. We could either have a casual conversation here and now, or I could wait until Monday, and have you meet me at the Sheriff's station, and we could talk in an interrogation room. Which do you prefer?" Detective Wisely quickly took off her boxing gloves and told Sarah straight.

A look of surprise quickly showed on Sarah's face, as if no one had ever spoken to her that way before.

"Fine, what do you want to know?" Sarah accepted her defeat and agreed to speak to Detective Wisely.

"Thank you, Sarah. Now, do you remember a classmate by the name of David Youngblood?"

"Of course I do. The kid who ran away during our sophomore year. What about him?"

"First, Davie did not just 'run away,' he was murdered. Would you know anything about his murder?"

"Davie, was murdered? That can't be true. That is not what I was told. I was told he ran always," Sarah's tone quickly changed.

"And who told you Davie ran away?"

Sarah sat for a moment, then repeated the question to Detective Wisely.

"Who told me Davie ran away? I am not sure who told me he ran away. I just heard it around school," Sarah replied to the question while avoiding contact with Brenda.

Brenda knew right then she was on the right track. She knew Sarah was hiding something and Brenda was going to get it out of Sarah.

"I find it hard to believe Sarah. You know exactly who told you that, but you are afraid to tell me. Why are you so scared, Sarah? Did you have something to do with his murder?" Brenda quickly dug into Sarah.

"How dare you accuse me of murdering Davie. I could never hurt anyone," Sarah shockingly replied to Detective Wisely.

"I am not accusing you of anything right now except for lying to me. I want to know who told you Davie ran away?"

Sarah became agitated and began twisting a lock of her long, blonde hair before answering the question.

"Chris told me, all right? It was Chris. He said Davie and him got into a fight and Davie told Chris he couldn't stay at the school anymore and was going to run away, so when Davie disappeared, I assumed he ran away. You don't think Chris murdered Davie, do you?" Sarah was fishing for information of her own.

"No, I did not say I suspected anyone at this time. I just said I wanted to speak to you about David Youngblood. Do you think Chris could be capable of committing such a brutal murder?" Brenda wanted to make sure Sarah didn't leave their interview thinking Chris was a suspect. Brenda knew if word got out about Chris, Sheriff Harper would shut her case down.

Sarah and Brenda took a moment in silence so both could relax, so they could just have a casual conversation.

"Sarah, I am not accusing anyone of anything right now. I just want to find out what happened to Davie. He deserves that, don't you think? Especially after the way all of you treated him. Calling his names and bullying him just because of a rumor," Brenda hoped Sarah had some empathy for Davie.

"I'm sorry, Detective, that is all I am going to say. I feel bad enough thinking about how I treated Davie in school, but I didn't kill him. I am done answering your questions, so I am going to go back to the reunion. At least there, people want to see me for me, not because of my past," Sarah informed Detective Wisely of her decision to stop answering her questions and quickly walked away.

Brenda was not surprised at Sarah's reaction, but she was not going to let her temper tantrum stop her from conducting her investigation. Brenda pulled out the list of names she wrote down to interview at the reunion and proceeded to gather up her next interviewee.

Brenda continued her questioning of each person she wanted to speak to before ending the night herself. She received the same information from each person she spoke to. Everyone told her that Chris was Davie's biggest bully and that they even bullied Davie because of the rumors Chris started. None of them were proud of the past behavior, but they all insisted it was not them, meaning Brenda was able to leave the reunion with an actual suspect in mind, Christopher Wooden.

Brenda got home a little after ten, which meant Dalton was already in bed, or some she expected. When she walked through her front door, she was surprised to see Dalton was still up and even prepared a late dinner for her. Brenda was so happy Dalton did all of that for her she ran over to Dalton and gave him the biggest hug he ever had. Dalton was a little shocked his mom was being so affectionate right then, but that didn't stop him from hugging her back just as tight.

After Brenda finished her late dinner and talking about life with Dalton, they both said their good nights and parted ways, each going to their bedrooms. Brenda was ready to get out of her clothes and go to bed. Brenda was exhausted from all the talking during the night and she was able to fall asleep quickly.

Robert Starnes

Chapter 9

Davie's Autopsy

A few days after the class reunion and Brenda's interrogations, she received a call from the coroner, Davie's autopsy reports were ready. With the news from the coroner, Brenda made a trip to the morgue to meet with Dr. Wexler, the town coroner. Brenda pulled up in front of the city morgue and after she was parked, she made her way inside the morgue and down to the basement. The basement is where all the bodies were stored until they were released to be buried.

As she walked inside the cold basement room, where Dr. Wexler was waiting for her, she suddenly was overwhelmed by the smell of death in the room. Quickly Brenda covered her nose before she spoke to the Dr.

"Dr. Wexler, what is that smell? Do you have fresh bodies down here?" Brenda asked in a high-pitched voice as he held her nose.

"Yes, sorry about the smell, we just had a couple come in from the accident on highway 48. It was a pretty nasty scene. Here, this is Vicks Vapor rub you can put under your nose to ease the smell," Dr. Wexler informed Brenda as she handed over a small blue jar of Vicks.

"Thank you. Now, you said you had the autopsy reports regarding Davies' death. What can you tell me?" Brenda quickly went into detective mode.

"Yes. I have his reports. There is not a lot I can tell you about his death, but there are some significant findings on his bones which tell of a horrific tell. While I was unable to determine his cause of death, I can tell you about what he may have gone through at the time of his death," Dr. Wexler related to Brenda.

"What can you tell me? I will take all you got if it gets me closer to finding his murder," Brenda pleaded with Dr. Wexler.

"I can tell you about the injuries Davie incurred at the time of his death. After examining his remains, I can say with certainty, Davie was brutally victimized at his time of death. The unhealed brakes to bones in his arms and legs suggest they happened very close to time of death. Also, there are several large skull fractures that never healed. He also had an orbital fracture on his face. By the looks of those fractures, I don't believe Davie could have survived such damaging head trauma. He was beaten to death. I can assure you of this," Dr. Wexler concluded her findings with Brenda.

Hearing about the injuries Davie had to endure before his death broke Brenda's heart. She could assume his death was total hell for him. Davie dying was actual mercy for what had been inflicted upon him. She was not prepared to have to explain Davie's death in full detail to his grieving mother June, but she knew she had to tell her the truth, but it was not going to be that day.

Brenda was now ready to dig in as much as she could into Christopher's life. She wanted to know everything he had done in the past and present. She needed hard evidence that Christopher murdered Davie, but she needed to figure out how to get the truth out of Chris. She knew there was no forensic evidence from the skeletal remains could link Davie's death to Chris, she needed to find another way. She just was not sure of how to get the evidence she needed, but she would find a way.

Brenda thanked Dr. Wexler for her report and saw herself outside of the morgue. She was ready for some fresh air after being down for even such a brief time. She could not understand how someone like Dr. Wexler could work in such conditions, but she silently thought about how thankful she was for people like Dr. Wexler.

By the time Brenda made it to her car, the smell of death was almost completely out of our senses, which she was thankful for. She jumped into her car and began to head to her office at the Sheriff's station. She wanted to continue going over her recorded interviews from the class reunion and putting them down on paper for her reports. While she was listening to the recordings and transcribing them into words, she couldn't help but think about how so many of Chris's classmates were friends with him just because of his father's position at the bank. Brenda couldn't fathom how people could just like someone because they hold a prominent position in a job. She wondered what made them so special, their own children were treated differently like they were above the law.

While Brenda was in the middle of re-listening to Sarah's interview, she felt Sarah knew more than she let on. Brenda thought it was time to get Sarah into the station for a more in-depth interrogation with her. Brenda decided it was time to contact Sarah and see if she could get her to voluntarily come to the station for some more questions. And if she refused, Brenda was ready to go to her office to question her in front of her employees, to Brenda, either way was acceptable.

Brenda arrived at the station and walked into her small office and began looking up phone numbers for Sarah. Once she found Sarah's contact information, she proceeded to call her cell phone. Sarah answered her call, which surprised Brenda.

"Hello, is this Sarah Wright?" Brenda asked the woman on the other end of the line.

"Yes, this is Sarah, who is asking?" Sarah replied.

"This is Detective Wisely from Whispering Pines. I am calling you to see if you have some time available coming up so you could come here to the station for some follow-up questions," Brenda explained her reason for calling.

"Sorry, Detective, but I think I made myself clear at the reunion, I am done answering your questions," Sarah shot back at Brenda from her request.

"No problem, Sarah. If you can't make time to come here to the station, I can always make myself available to come to your office and do the formal interview there. Just let me know which you would prefer," Brenda expressed to Sarah she really wanted to speak to her, one way or another.

The line was quiet for a moment before Sarah responded.

"There is no reason to come to my office. Let me check my schedule and get back to you when I have a free day to come there. Is that acceptable?" Sarah suddenly reconsidered speaking to Brenda.

"That is perfectly fine with me, but don't take too long to get back to me. I want to get this out of the way as quickly as possible so I can continue with my investigation," Brenda stipulated to Sarah before hanging up the call.

When their call ended, Brenda knew it would be a couple of days before Sarah called her back to confirm a time and date for her to come back to Whispering Pines for an official interview. Since she had time on her hands, we thought it would be good for her to go back to the crime scene. Brenda knew it was a long shot, but she knew it wouldn't hurt just to look.

Brenda left her office and headed out to Mr. Brown's land, back to the well Davie's remains were found in. She was not sure of what she would be looking for, but it was worth doing. While driving out to Klienstown, Brenda took time to appreciate all the beauty the country life had to offer. The trees were all lush and green with wildflowers growing all along the country roads. Brenda was enjoying the sights so long she did not realize she made it to Klienstown.

After Brenda snapped out of her trance, she saw the county road which led to the crime scene. Making a quick right and slowing down for the gravel road, she creeped along until she was at the entrance to Mr. Brown's land with the well on it. She knew she did not have to ask Mr. Brown's permission to enter, as it was an active crime scene, but she figured it wouldn't be long before he showed up. With that in mind, Brenda got out of her car and proceeded to unlock the gate so she could drive in. Once she was inside the gate, she put her car in park and got out to close the gate behind her. She was not sure if Mr. Brown had farm animals in the pasture, so she wanted to close the gate just in case.

With the gate closed, Brenda drove her car a little deeper into the pasture and parked just outside the crime tape. Brenda exited her car, grabbed a bag from the back seat of the car, and headed over to the well. She was ready to begin her search for clues as to how Davie's body ended up in the well in the first place.

Standing beside the well, Brenda placed her bag down and grabbed a flashlight out of it. She wanted to see if there could be some type of evidence down in the well. She signed her bright LED flashlight down into the well and was able to see sticks and trash down in it. She was curious how a few bags of trash could end up in the well and the person who threw them in didn't notice Davie's body or smell his decomposing body as they threw their trash over into the well. She knew then she had to go down into the well to retrieve the bags of trash with hopes she may find out whose trash it was.

Brenda switched off the flashlight and bent down to grab a long, thick rope out of her bag. With the rope in hand, she walked over to her vehicle and tied one end of the rope to the back trailer hitch on the back of it. Once the rope was tied down, she walked back over to the well and tossed the other end over the side and watched the rope fall until it reached the bottom of the well. Brenda was surprised at how deep the well was, but she knew she had to go down to the bottom. With the rope set, Brenda reached back into her bag and pulled out rope clamps she would use to lower herself down into the well as well as to use to climb back up.

With all her gear set, Brenda attached the clamps to the rope and sat on the edge of the well, dangling her legs over the side inside the well. With caution, Brenda steadied herself with the rope clamps and began to ease her entire body over into the well. She had a tight grip on the clamps and extended her legs straight out and eased her body down until her legs were parallel to her body. She continued to take a step down the side of the well, while lowering herself at the same time. She kept up her momentum until she was close enough to the bottom for her to grab one of the bags of trash. Brenda stopped her descent and grabbed the remaining rope and wrapped it around her backside and back up to her hands. She created a swing for herself, enabling her to be able to release one of the rope clamps so she could grab a trash bag. After Brenda had the bag in her hand, she secured it to a hook she had attached to a belt she was wearing. With the bag secure, she reached back down and grabbed another bag, repeating her earlier steps until it was secure on a hook as well. With the bags secure, Brenda grabbed the rope clamp and started to work her way back up to the top of the well, with two trash bags in tow.

As Brenda was climbing back to the top of the well, she noticed a shadow cover her view. At first, she was not sure what it could be causing the shadow, but it didn't take her long before she heard a familiar voice yelling down to her.

"What are you doing down there?" Mr. Brown questioned Brenda.

"Mr. Brown, is that you?" Brenda replied.

"Yes ma'am. Now, why are you on my property?"

"I will tell you when I get out of the well. Do you mind giving me a hand?" Brenda asked Mr. Brown.

"Well, since you were able to get onto my property and lower yourself down into my well, I think you are more than capable of getting yourself out of the well. I'll just wait here for you," Mr. Brown did not seem happy about having someone on his land without his permission.

Brenda watched as the shadow moved out of her view of the well entrance and continued to make her way, slowly, to the opening of the well. It took her another ten minutes until she reached the top. Once she was at the opening, she grabbed one bag of trash off the hook on one side of her belt and threw it over and out of the well. She repeated the same step with the other bag of trash before she was able to pull herself out and over the top of the well.

Brenda was out of breath by the time she got out of the well and waited to take a moment to catch her breath before she spoke to Mr. Brown. But Mr. Brown was not patient.

"Now, what are you doing on my land? And what's with the bags of trash?" Mr. Brown began his questioning again.

"Can I have a minute, I just climbed down your well and back out. I need a minute, please?" Brenda expressed to Mr. Brown.

"I would be inclined to give you a minute, if you would have asked my permission before trespassing on my land."

"Fine! First, Mr. Brown, this is an active crime scene and I do not have to get your permission to visit the site. Second, I noticed those trash bags at the bottom of your well, as you stated, which is the same place you found Davie's skeletal remains. I want to know how someone could just throw trash into your well and never notice there was a dead body, or skeletal remains, at the bottom of it. Would you like to explain that to me?" Brenda instantly barked back at Mr. Brown.

Mr. Brown was silent for a moment and was looking as if he didn't want to answer the Detective's question.

"People pay me for the use of my wells for their garbage. I have several unused wells on my land, so I am not sure who exactly uses which well. Maybe the trash was thrown into this well after the bones were found and removed. Do you think that could be possible?" Mr. Brown had an excuse for everything.

"If that's the case, then they broke the law by contaminating a crime scene. This caution tape has been up since you found his remains, so now I really want to know whose trash it is," Brenda finally found a way to stop Mr. Brown's excuses.

Mr. Brown had nothing else to say to the Detective and decided to walk back over to his truck and sit down on his open tailgate. From there, Mr. Brown watched as Brenda opened the bags of trash and began sifting through them. One bag at a time. She noticed she would pull out magazines, envelopes, and receipts from the bags. Mr. Brown continued to sit and watch the events unfold right in front of him and dared not to interrupt her work. After fifteen minutes of watching Brenda dig through the trash, he noticed she suddenly stopped digging, as if she found what she was looking for.

Brenda grabbed a few things she found in the trash and walked over to her car and placed them inside her car, sitting on the front passenger seat. Then she walked to the back of her car and opened the truck. With the trunk of her car open, she walked back over to the area with the bags of strewn trash on the ground, carefully placed all it back into the bags, and carried them over and placed them in the trunk and shut the lid.

With Brenda having all she thought she needed, she walked to the front drivers' side of her car, opened the door, and looked over at Mr. Brown.

"I'm done now, so if you would kindly open the gate for me, I can leave. And thanks for your help, it will be noted in my report," Brenda snapped at Mr. Brown.

Without anything more to say, Mr. Brown got up from the tailgate and walked back to the gate. After the gate was opened, Brenda proceeded to drive right past Mr. Brown, giving him a sarcastic wave and she passed by him.

Brenda was excited about her findings from inside the well and could not wait to get back to her office to dig a little more into the trash. She knew she was on to something and was ready to keep going.

Chapter 10

Confronting Christopher

It took Brenda a few days to go through all the trash she found down in the well on Mr. Brown's land, the same well Davie's remains were found in. Some items she found inside the trash were receipts from the local grocery store, old magazines with the label party intact, old bills from the person who threw away the trash, and old fast-food bags and drinks. She needed some more time so she could confirm what she found came from the address listed on the bills before she would make an arrest.

Before Brenda could begin her day looking for more concrete proof of who the trash belonged to, she was notified by dispatch that she had a visitor at the station. Wondering who was there to see her, she replied 10-4 to dispatch and headed back to the station.

Upon arriving at the station Brenda noticed a new BMW sitting out front, she suddenly figured out who was there to visit her. It was Sarah, one of Davie's previous classmates she interviewed at the class reunion. Brenda entered the station with a serious look on her face when she came face-to-face with Sarah again.

"Glad to see you could make time to speak to me, Sarah," Detective Wisely sarcastically said to her guest.

"Well, it's not like I had an option. Now that I am here, what do you want to talk about?" Sarah angrily replied.

"Please, come with me to the interrogation room, where we can have a bit more privacy," Detective Wisely instructed Sarah.

Sarah complied and followed the detective back to a private room. Upon entering the room, Sarah noticed how stale and bare the room looked and mumbled something under her breath.

"Did you say something?" Detective Wisely quickly replied.

"No, I didn't say anything. Now, where would you like me to sit?" Sarah quickly responded.

"Take a set here," Detective Wisely pulled back one of the metal chairs which lined the table on both sides.

Sarah did as she was told and took a seat. Once she was settled, Detective Wisely began her questioning.

"Now, you told me Chris informed you Davie ran away when she spoke at the class reunion, correct?"

"Yes, that is what I said, and it is the truth."

"Great, now did you hear any rumors about Davie which would have started the summer before your freshman year of high school?"

"Yes, maybe. It's so hard to remember everything I may have heard over ten years ago. Can you refresh my memory as to what may have been said about him?"

"Stop lying to me Sarah, you know exactly what rumors I am talking about. Now, did you spread any of the rumors yourself, or make any of them up?"

"Fine, yes, I heard rumors that Davie was gay, but I didn't start them and before you ask, no I didn't hear them from any students at school. I heard my parents talking about it one day before I left to meet up with Tammy Faye. What do rumors have to do with his murder?"

"That is what I am trying to figure out. Do you know why your parents were talking about Davie being gay?"

"No, I don't know why they said it, or who they heard it from, but I heard it from them for the first time. I would suggest you ask them, but if you have done your due diligence, you would already know both of my parents are dead. My mother died of cancer three years ago and my father drank himself to death after my mother died. So, you will just have to believe me this time, Detective Wisely," with an emphasis on 'Detective Wiseley.' Now, is there anything else I can answer for you?"

"If that is all you have, then I have no more questions for you. Thank you for coming in, you are free to leave now," Detective Wisely ended her questions for Sarah.

Even though Sarah claimed her parents were talking about Davie's sexual orientation and could not find out who they heard it from, still made her wonder, who told them that and why? Instead of spending more time on questions she could not get answers for, she felt it was time to get back to finding out whose trash she found in the well.

Brenda decided she wanted to start at the local grocery store. Since she had the receipts, which had a time and date stamped on them, she wanted to see if the store had security cameras. Brenda parked her car and made her way inside the small store. She began to walk around the store first to look for any signs of cameras. As he walked down the aisles, she was not pleased by the lack of cameras. She felt she may not be able to retrieve any useful information from the store. That was until she went to check out and noticed there was one camera in the store, it was located right about the only exit door. Brenda was filled with hope once again.

After checking out, Brenda asked the employee who checked her out if she could speak to the manager. The cashier turned around in her station and knocked on a plexiglass window directly behind her. It was to the manager's office.

"He's in there," the cashier told Brenda while pointing behind herself.

"Thank you. Is this the door?" Brenda asked as she walked past the cashier to a door leading to the box that made up the manager's office.

"Yep," the cashier replied as she turned to help the next customer in line.

Before Brenda could knock on the door, it was opened by the occupant inside. Brenda assumed they must be the manager, since they were in the office, so she began asking him some questions.

"I'm sorry to bother you, but does that security camera work?" Brenda asked as she pointed to the camera about the exit door.

"Oh that? No, it's just for show. We don't have any real security cameras here. We are a small town, and we know everyone here," the manager explained.

"You may know everyone here in town, but it's obvious you don't trust them all, or you wouldn't have a fake security camera posted at the exit," Brenda pointed out to the unsuspecting manager.

"Now I didn't say that. Those cameras are more for folks from out of town who come here to watch the football games. We don't have any problems here with theft.

Brenda gave the manager a disappointed look and thanked him for his time. She turned around and exited the store with her hope depleted. Brenda knew she had a few other resources she could use to get the confirmation she needed regarding the bags of trash.

Brenda knew it was time to hit up the post office. She knew the postmaster could scan the part of the labels of the old magazine to get the full address. She was hoping she wouldn't have to go that route because of how small the town is, once the postmaster scanned the magazines and the identity of who they belonged to could get out, and she did not want to risk it in the beginning. But without video evidence of the receipts, she had no other option to make sure the trash came from her suspect's home.

Brenda pulled up to the only post office in town and walked inside. As she walked in, she noticed a few locals inside checking their post office boxes, so she stood back and waited for them to leave. Once she knew the place was empty, except for her and the postmaster, she made her say up to the counter.

"Excuse me. Are you the postmaster?" Brenda casually inquired.

"Yes, I am the postmaster here. What can I do for you?" the clerk responded.

"Hello, I am detective Wisely and I am here to ask for your help. I am working on a littering case and wanted to see if you could look something up for me? I hate people who litter all over this lovely town," Brenda decided to change her tactics on why she needed the information, so if it did get out, it would only be because someone was a litterbug.

"It's nice to meet you Detective, my name is Suzy and I have been the postmaster here for almost fifty years and I hate litterbugs. Folks need to help do their part in keeping Whispering Pines a beautiful place to live. So, what can I do to help you?"

"I am glad to hear you love this place as much as I do. I was wondering if you would be able to scan the barcode of an old magazine I found. The address and name of the purchaser were removed, but there is a postal barcode on it," Brenda asked Suzy.

"You bet I can, do you have the magazine you would like me to scan?"

"Yes, here you go," Brenda told Suzy as she handed the magazine over to her.

"I'll be right back. I need a minute to get the address and I'll be right back."

Suzy took the magazine to the back of the post office while Brenda waited for her to come back. It was not long before Suzy came back to Brenda with a piece of paper in her hand.

"Here you go, Detective. I hate to admit it but it's a, local, residents' trash you found. It is so upsetting to know Mr. Wooden, the president of the bank, litters here. He should be so ashamed."

"Thank you, Suzy. Do you mind keeping this between us? I don't want to tarnish a good man's name over a bag of trash. I'm sure when I speak to him, he will not litter anymore here in Whispering Pines," Brenda hoped Suzy would understand her concerns and knowing how much power Mr. Wooden has in Whispering Pines, Brenda hoped she would not tell anyone about the little bug.

"You have nothing to worry about. I would never tell a soul about Mr. Wooden's litter problem. I value my job way too much to get involved with anything he has going on," Suzy replied to Brenda, which let her know Suzy understood the assignment and would not utter a word.

Now that Brenda had two pieces of evidence from the trash that both lead back to Christopher's father, she knew it was time for her to call Christopher down to the station for some hard questioning.

Brenda got back to the station and walked straight back to her office. After she was inside her office, she shut the door behind herself. She wanted some privacy as she made a call to Christopher. Brenda picked up her office phone and dialed Chris's phone number. The line rang a couple of times before it was answered.

"Hello, who is this?" Chris answered the call.

"Hello Chris, this is Detective Wisely. I am calling to see if you could come down to the station today for a few more questions."

"Is this about Davie's case?"

"In a manner of speaking, it is. Is it going to be a problem for you?" Brenda questioned Chris.

"Not at all, what time would you like me there?"

"How about now? Is that going to be a problem?"

"Not at all, I was just about to leave my parents' house. You see, we have dinner here every Friday. I will be there in fifteen minutes, if that is okay with you?"

"Fifteen minutes is perfect. Do you mind if I have Davie's mothers here during the questioning?" Brenda felt compelled to ask.

"Not at all, please have June come to the station as well. I have nothing to hide," Chris quickly responded to Brenda.

"Perfect. I'm sure she would love to see you, since you were Davies' best friend and all. I know you hung out quite a bit at their house many years ago. She just adores Davies' friends. They are the only connection she has to Davie these days," Brenda played it off as it was going to be nothing more than a casual conversation at the station before handing up with Chris.

Brenda ended the call with Chris and at once called June, Davies' mother. She wanted to have June present during Chris's questioning, hoping she would be enough to get the truth from Chris. He and Davie were best friends before Chris moved so unexpectedly after the summer before their freshman year of high school.

June quickly answered the phone, as if she was expecting Davie to be calling, and was surprised Detective Wisely was asking her to join her in questioning Christopher Wooden at the station.

"You want me there while you question him? Why are you questioning Chris anyway? He was Davies' best friend before he went missing. I mean before he was killed. Sorry, I keep forgetting Davie is dead and never coming home again. It has been a lot to process after all these years of hoping and waiting for him to come home to me," June expressed heartache as she replied to Brenda's request.

"I understand June, you have nothing to apologize for. I think Chris would be more comfortable speaking freely with you present. I know it is a lot to ask, but I could really use your help," Brenda pleaded with June to attend the interview with Chris.

June took a few minutes to think about what Brenda was asking of her, but then decided she would do whatever she could to help find out who killed her beloved son, Davie.

"Yes, I will be there. Give me ten minutes."

June ended the call with Brenda and began to get ready to head to the police station. June did not know what to expect while talking with Chris, but she felt deep down Brenda would not be asking for her help unless she truly needed it. June grabbed her purse, ran out to her car, and headed to the station to meet up with Brenda.

As Brenda waited for June and Chris to arrive at the station, she went into the interrogation room to make sure the recording devices were all up and running. She wanted to make sure every word spoken during the interview was recorded. She had a feeling they would be getting the answers to all their questions answered soon enough.

June arrived first to the station and was greeted by Brenda, so she quickly thanked her for agreeing to attend the interview and escorted her back to the interrogation room. Once June was all set, Brenda went back to the entrance of the station to wait for Chris to arrive.

It wasn't long before Chris arrived at the station and to Brenda's surprise, he had his father with him, Mr. Wooden, the bank president. Brenda had a sense she may be on the right track if Chris needed his father with him during the interview.

As Chris and his father entered the police station, Brenda greeted them both and asked if Mr. Wooden wouldn't mind waiting in the sitting area of the station while she spoke to Chris alone.

"I'm sorry, but if you are going to speak to my son, I am going to have to demand I be present during the interview," Mr. Wooden demanded of Brenda.

"I'm also sorry, sir, but your son is an adult and unless you are his attorney, I am going to have to insist you stay out here. If anything comes up and we require your assistance, you will be the first to know,' Brenda shot down Mr. Wooden's demands.

"Do you know who you are speaking to, Detective? I am the president of the bank, and my family has contributed large amounts of money for this city, and I will not be spoken to like this."

"I know exactly who you are and what your status is in the town. Regardless, you are not required, nor permitted to sit in the room with us during an investigation. Do you understand?" Brenda factually told Mr. Wooden.

"How dare you speak to me. I want to speak to…" Mr. Wooden was quickly cut off by Sheriff Harper.

"I am right here, Mr. Wooden, and like the detective told you, you will have to wait out here."

"Is that the way you are going to play this? I hope you understand, my family, nor myself, will forget this."

"Noted, now, Detective Wisely, could you please escort Christopher back to the interrogation room and begin your interview," Sheriff Harper asked Brenda, who was in total shock of him standing up for her to Mr. Wooden.

Brenda thanked the Sheriff and escorted Chris back to the interrogation room, where June was patiently waiting. As soon as Chris entered the room and noticed Davies' mother, June, sitting there too, she quickly lowered his head as if he was ashamed of something.

"Take a seat Chris. As you know, I am here to question you about David Youngblood's death. You already know his mother, June, so if you could just take a seat, this will all be over soon," Brenda instructed Chris.

Chris took a seat across the table from June and glanced up to her.

"It's good to see you Mrs. Youngblood. How have you been?" Chris spoke softly to June.

"How have I been? Did you just ask me that? How do you think I have been doing? I thought my son ran away because of something I may have done for all these years, just to find out he never left Whispering Pines. He was murdered and thrown down a well like garbage. How do you think I feel?" June held nothing back as she answered Chris.

Before Chris could respond to June, he quickly lowered his head back down and began to cry. It was obvious to Brenda there was more to Chris's side of the story, one she was ready to hear.

"Chris, you know why you are here, correct?" Brenda asked before she began her questioning.

"Yes ma'am. You want to question me about Davies murder," Chris replied in a sobbing voice.

"That is correct. Now, before I begin questioning you, I need to read you your Miranda Rights, do you understand? It is just a procedure before we question anyone about a case. It does not mean you are under arrest, you are just here to answer some questions," Brenda informed Chris.

"I understand," Chris acknowledged.

"Good. You have the right to remain silent. Anything you say can and will be used against you in a court of law. You have the right to an attorney. If you cannot afford an attorney, one will be appointed for you. Do you understand your rights I have just read to you," Brenda asked Chris.

"Yes, I underhand my rights. I have nothing to hide," Chris answered Brenda.

"Great, so you are willing to answer some questions without an attorney present?"

"Yes, I just want to get this over with."

"If at any time you feel you need an attorney, all you must do is ask for one and the questioning will stop. Knowing this, are you still agreeing to speak to us now?"

"Yes, I will answer all of your questions to the best of my ability."

"Great. Now, what exactly was your relationship with Davie, during the summer before your freshman year? Why did you stop being his friend?"

"You must understand how living in a small town is before I can answer the question. There are some things you can't do in a small town, or a certain type of person. I loved Davie with all my heart. He was my best friend since kindergarten, and I didn't want to lose him as a friend, but I had no choice."

"What do you mean, you had no choice but to stop being his friend?"

"I don't feel comfortable saying it in front of Mrs. Youngblood," Chris expressed.

"It's okay, Chris. I want to hear the truth, that is all," June spoke to reassuring Chris she was okay with whatever he had to say.

Chris sat for a moment with his head in his hand as he cried. Brenda could tell something was different about the way Chris was crying. It was not because he killed Davie, but because he genuinely loved him, and he was grieving.

"Chris, I know this may be hard to talk about, but it is obvious you deeply cared for Davie. You have been carrying around this burden for so long now, it will only help you if you let it out. It's time for the truth, Chris," Brenda gently pulled at Chris's emotions.

"I didn't kill Davie and I didn't move away because of Davie. I had to move. I had no choice once my father caught us together," Chris began to explain the past events in his life. "I loved Davie with all my heart. We were not just best friends, but he was my boyfriend. We had been together for several years before my father caught us kissing one night in my room, when Davie stayed over. He barged into my room unannounced and as soon as he opened my bedroom door, he became furious. He started yelling at us and accusing Davie of forcing himself on me. We were about to be fifteen and starting high school and I didn't know what to do, so I let my father think that was what happened."

"Chris, I am so sorry your father did that to you both. I can't imagine what you must have been thinking at the time. I'm sure it was very traumatic for you both. What happened after your father caught you together?" June spoke from the heart at Chris.

"I'm so sorry, Mrs. Youngblood. I truly am. After my father saw us together, he demanded for Davie to leave our house and never come back. Davie was too afraid to call you and tell you what happened, my father chose to drive Davie home that night. After my father returned home, he told me I was not allowed to see Davie again and I was going to have to move to live with my mother, until things died down. I never wanted to be away from Davie, and I never started any rumors about Davie. That was all my dad's doings. He made it a habit of telling any parent of our classmates that Davie was gay, and they could keep their children away from him. I didn't know any of this until I returned to town, in the middle of our sophomore year. When I found out what my father had done to Davie, I reached out to Davie. I told him I needed to see him. So, we made plans to meet at the bonfire on Mr. Brown's land in December, before the holiday break," Chris began to let it all out.

"What happened at the bonfire, Chris?" Brenda needed to know.

"I didn't know it at the time, but my father found out I reached out to Davie, so he volunteered to be a parent at the event. Davie and I met up just a little way away from the bonfire and began to talk. I told him I never started any rumors about him and that I still loved him dearly, but since I had just come back to live with my father, if we were ever going to make it as a couple, we would have to do it in secret. Davie understood and agreed with me. Right after we had an agreement, I leaned in to kiss Davie at the same time my father came around the corner and saw me kissing Davie. He became so furious, the next thing I knew, my father picked up a large tree branch that was laying on the ground and struck Davie in the head with hit. He just kept hitting Davie repeatedly, until he stopped moving. All I could do was stand there and watch my dad beat Davie to death," Chris began crying even harder as he described the events that took place right in front him and he couldn't do anything about it.

"Oh, Chris, I am so sorry you had to witness something so horrible and to someone you loved. I don't know what to say that could ease your pain, but I want you to know that knowing you were with Davie during his last breathes gives me some peace. Knowing he was not alone when he died. He was with someone he loved who loved him back," June slowly wiped tears from her own eyes and she reached over the table and took hold of Chris's hands.

"I didn't know what to do at the time. Looking back now, I wish I would have jumped in front of Davie and let my dad beat me instead. My life has never been the same since that day. It's all my fault Davie is dead. All because we loved each other and my dad couldn't handle having a gay son, not here in Whispering Pines," Chris let his guilt out.

"What happened after your father stopped hitting Davie?" Brenda needed to know how Davie ended up in the well.

"When my dad stopped hitting Davie, he turned and told me he was not about to have a faggot for a son, and demanded to never let my feelings get out of control and focus on getting married. Then he composed himself enough to pick Davie's body up and he knew there was a well close by, because we threw our trash in it with Mr. Brown's permission. So, he walked over to the well, which was about a hundred feet from where we were. As soon as he got to the well, he threw Davie's body into it and made me go back to get the log he used to kill him with and throw it in as well. After Davie was in the well, my dad told me if I ever told anyone about what happened, not only would he go to jail, but so would I and I had to think about my future. So, that is what I did. I never told anyone about what happened that night and have had to live with this from them on. It was the worst mistake of my life, and I am terribly sorry. I hope you can forgive me Mrs. Youngblood. I am telling you the truth about our love, it was real and still is for me," Chris reached his hands out for Junes, who openly accepted his apology and understood why he could tell anyone about it.

With the end of the interview, Chris stood up and walked over to June and gave her a big hug before Brenda had to interrupt them both so she could place Chris under arrest. Chris understood why Brenda had to arrest him and didn't resist. Once Chris was in handcuffs, Brenda escorted him out of the room and back to the holding cells, before going back to the waiting area to place Mr. Wooden under arrest as well.

Chapter 11

The Community's Reaction

It did not take long before word got out about Mr. Wooden, the bank's president, was arrested. Sheriff Harper knew it would only be a short amount of time before the locals of Whispering Pines began calling the station to try and get more information about the arrest. Sheriff Harper had already informed his staff of officers and dispatchers not to give out any information to the caller. Even though Mr. Wooden was arrested, he knew there still had to be a trial, so he wanted to give a little time before the local paper caught wind of the arrest as well. Once the news hit the paper, it would answer all the questions they may have.

Brenda was extremely satisfied knowing there were arrests made in David Youngblood's case. However, she was saddened about Christophers arrest because he was only a child when it happened and he was afraid of his father, just like many of the locals of Whispering Pines were. She had already planned to speak to the District Attorney regarding any charges which could be brought against Chris. She felt he had been punished for over ten years with his guilt for not being able to help Davie, his one true love, all because of his homophobic father. Brenda was prepared to suggest Chris to be tried as a minor, since he was only sixteen at the time when his father beat Davie to death.

Another concern Sheriff Harper was worried about was if it would be possible for Mr. Wooden to even have a fair trial in Whispering Pines, so he was prepared to suggest to the District Attorney for a change of venue for the trial. He felt there were either too many residents who were afraid to go against Mr. Wooden if selected for the jury, or there were too many residents who were so afraid of Mr. Wooden they would find him guilty just to make sure he never interfered in their business again. Either outcome seemed to be to be a definite guilty verdict to come out of the trial, but he still felt it would not be a fair trial.

Sheriff Harper wanted to see if Detective Wisely would like to go to the office of the District Attorney.

"Detective, you mentioned you wanted to speak to the D.A. about Christopher. I also have concerns about a trial here in Whispering Pines and I wanted to ask if you wanted to head over to the DA's office with me?" Sheriff Harper asked Brenda.

"Absolutely! What time are you planning to go?" Brenda inquired.

"Now, if you are available."

"I'm ready, lead the way, Sheriff."

Sheriff Harper walked out of the station, with Brenda in tow, and over to his cruiser. Once they were both inside the car, Sheriff Harper started making their way over to the courthouse, where the DA's office is located. As they arrived, Sheriff Harper parked his car right out front at the courthouse entrance. After parking the car, the Sheriff and Detective Wisely, both stepped out of the car and made their way into the courthouse. As it was Detective Wisely's first time at the courthouse, she followed Sheriff Harper up the stairs, through the front door, and along the hallway until he stopped at the office door of the D.A.

The D.A. was surprised to see the Sheriff and new detective entering her office unscheduled.

"Sheriff, do we have a meeting scheduled for today?" D.A. Parker inquired of his visitors.

"No, Sir. Now, as you are aware, we have arrested Mr. Wooden and his son Christopher for the murder David Youngblood, but we have some questions and concerns to speak to you about," Sheriff Harper insisted to D.A. Parker.

"I see. And you must be Detective Wisely, the newest member of Whispering Pines police department. Come in and have a seat, it just so happens I have some free time this morning," D.A. Parker agreed to meet with the pair of them.

"Yes, Sir. You may call me Brenda and thank you for agreeing to see us without an appointment," Brenda replied with gratitude.

Sheriff Harper motioned for Brenda to take a seat first, then after she was seated, he sat next to her in another open chair. D.A. Parker give them both a few minutes to get settled before inquiring about their questions and concerns.

"Now, what questions and concerns do you have about the Youngblood case?" D.A. Parker asked to create an open dialect from his guests.

"Detective Wisely, why don't you go first," Sheriff Harper suggested.

"Thank you, Sheriff. D.A. Parker, I am here today to speak to you about Christopher Wooden. From what I have been able to uncover during my investigation, I have a couple of questions about him," Brenda told D.A. Parker.

"What would you like to ask? I will answer what I can, but realize this being such a fresh case, and I have not been able to review all the information regarding this case at this time. Is this going to be an issue?"

"I understand, if you can't answer my question, you can take it as a suggestion on the matter of concern I have."

"I can do that, Brenda."

"Thank you. First, I want to ask if you would be trying Christopher as an adult?"

"Let me ask you, how would you like to see Christopher tried as and why?"

"I think if Christopher is going to be tried, I believe he should be tried as a minor. I know at the age of sixteen he can be tried as an adult, but I think there are some mitigating circumstances for Christopher. You see, he was only in the eighth grade when his father caught him, and the victim kissing and became upset about the incident. After the incident at their home, on Christophers first day of high school, his father forced him to move away to live with his mother. He was also instructed not to ever contact Davie again, or he would have hell to pay. As you may know, many of the residents of Whispering Pines are afraid of Mr. Wooden because of his position at the bank, can you imagine how scared Christopher must have been. I feel he had no choice but to obey his father," Brenda expressed to D.A. Parker.

"I have been able to review the interview you had with Christopher and know about the incident between him and the victim, but it does not explain why he never came forward with the truth. I read in your report that you met with Christopher twice, once at school and the second at the station. He could have come clean when you first met with him, but he didn't. Can you elaborate on your thoughts about the first interview?"

"Yes, I can. I believe Christopher was and still fears his father. I have read an article written by Bessel van der Kolk about how childhood trauma could cause the brain to constantly feel fear and danger. This suggests to me Christopher has felt fear believing he has always been in danger. In danger from his father, Mr. Wooden. With all of this in mind, I am requesting Christopher should speak to a psychiatrist to determine his state of mind, not only during the event of Davies murder, but also about his state of mind now to determine if he should be tried at all," Brenda ended her conversation with the plea to D.A. Parker not to charge Christopher for is part in Davies murder.

D.A. Parker sat back in his oversized brown leather chair across the other side of his desk from Brenda, closing his eyes to think. D.A. Parker took over ten minutes before he was ready to reply to Brenda.

"Brenda, I can see your point of view on this situation, and I will take it into account before issuing an arrest warrant on Christopher at this time. I will give Christopher the opportunity to speak to one of our psychiatrists and if they feel the same way you do, then I will agree to drop the charges against Christopher. Is this satisfactory with you?"

"Yes, thank you again. I have nothing more to ask," Brenda concluded her conversation with D.A. Parker, leaving time for Sheriff Harper to speak with the D.A.

"Now, Sheriff, what concerns do you have about the Youngblood case," D.A. switched his focus on the Sheriff.

Sheriff Harper expressed all his concerns he had about Mr. Wooden getting a fair trial in Whispering Pines and suggested D.A. Parker to put in for a change of venue. They spoke for thirty minutes before their conversation ended with no agreed upon conclusion. D.A. Parker said he would give it a thought, but he would more than likely not request a change of venue, because he had faith the good people of Whispering Pines could be jurors on the case and remain impartial while coming to a decision.

Sheriff Harper and Detective Wisely thanked D.A. Parker, who took time out of his day to meet with them, then exited his office and continued out of the courthouse until they were at the Sheriff's car. The Sheriff didn't have a look of satisfaction on his face, at least not like Brenda did, and he was not in a talking mood.

As they made their way back to the police station, Brenda could tell the Sheriff was really expecting the

D.A. to agree to the change of venue. She was not sure what she could say to him to make light of the situation, so she continued to ride with silence. The silent ride was only for a couple of miles, but it felt like a hundred miles to Brenda.

As soon as the Sheriff stopped his car at the station, Brenda quickly got out and waited for Sheriff Harper to get out before moving towards the station. She waited for a minute or two until she realized the Sheriff was not getting out of the car. Instead, he waved for her to go on to the station as he began to back out of his parking spot. Brenda felt he was up to something, but she didn't want to get involved with what he had going on in his head, so she turned and went into the station.

Brenda walked past dispatch and walked straight back to the station to the holding cells. Brenda was excited to get the paperwork started on getting Christopher released and let him know what she and the D.A. talked about. She didn't want to give Chris false hope, but he had a good feeling about what the outcome would be and releasing Christopher was the first step.

Brenda didn't want to discuss anything about the case in front of Mr. Wooden, so she took Chris out of the holding cell and took him back to her office. Brenda and Chris spoke for an hour before she took him back to his cell so she could begin working on his release papers. Brenda finished Chris' release paperwork and faxed it over to the court clerk's office. It took another two hours before Brenda was informed all Chris' paperwork was in order and was granted release. With his release granted, Brenda walked back to the holding cells and opened Chris' cell door and walked him back to the intake desk. With Chris being granted release, she still had to inform him not to leave town, because there were still a few things Chris would have to do to keep from being charged and tried in Davies case. Chris agreed to the terms of his release and decided he wanted to go home and get some rest. Brenda was at the end of her shift and made the same decision as Chris and headed home. She knew tomorrow would be another busy workday.

The next morning, Brenda was woken up by a loud knocking on her front door. It was unusual for Brenda to not only have guests, but especially a guest to come over before she was up. Brenda quickly jumped out of bed, put on her robe, and quickly made her way to the door. She hoped she could get the visitor to stop knocking on her door before she woke up Dalton.

Brenda instinctively swung her door open and was shocked to see her nosy neighbor, Joy, standing outside on her porch waving around a new paper. The first thing

Brenda thought of was information about Mr. Wooden and Christophers arrests had already hit the news, so she quickly asked Joy to bring down her voice before letting her in.

Joy lowered her voice and casually went inside Brenda's home and took a seat in the living room. Once Brenda felt Joy had calmed down, she wanted to know what brought Joy over to her house so early in the morning.

"Joy, do you know what time it is? Do you have an emergency?" Brenda questioned Joy.

"Yes, I know it's early, but this could not wait. While it may not be considered an emergency, I must know if the article in the Whispering Pines paper this morning is true?" Joy picked the paper in her hand up and pointed at it.

"I do not know what article you are talking about. I was asleep and did not receive the local paper. Now, what article are you asking about?" Brenda answered with a bit of annoyance in her tone.

"This one, right here!" Joy replied as she opened the paper and pointed again at an 'Breaking News' article on the front page of the paper. "It says you have arrested Mr. Wooden and his son Christopher for the murder of David Youngblood. Is it true? Did they kill the poor boy ten years ago?"

Brenda had no idea how someone found out about the arrests of the suspects. That was until after she read the article. When she finished reading it, she had a feeling she knew how the paper got their information, but she was not going to tell Joy about her suspicions.

"Joy, I am not allowed to speak about an ongoing investigation. I cannot confirm, or deny, if the article is true. Now, if you would please go home and let me go back to bed. I have a busy day scheduled for today," Brenda pleaded with Joy to let it go and go home.

Joy gave up trying to get anything out of Brenda, knowing she plays by the book, so she picked up her paper, apologized to Brenda about her early wake up visit, and walked out heading home.

Brenda knew at that moment her day was going to be worse than she expected. Every resident of Whispering Pines will know about the arrests and things could get out of control. So, she tried to shake it out of her mind and made her way back to her bedroom, lay down, and went back to sleep. For a few more hours at least.

Brenda woke up again to begin her day, still a little groggy from being woken up before the sun came up, took a quick shower, dressed for work, then left the house.

On Brenda's way to the station, she was surprised as she drove to the station, she noticed the entire town square was covered with parked cars. To her, it looked as if the entire town was there, and she had a feeling she knew why. After passing the square and turning on the road to the station, it was clear everyone must have received the morning paper. Brenda saw the large crowd of residents standing outside the station. She made her way past the residents in the street and parked her car, got out and proceeded into the station.

As Brenda approached the station, she made her way through the crowd and didn't respond to any of the questions being thrown at her by the crowd. She could tell the entire town was in uproar about the arrests, but she couldn't tell if it was because of Mr. Wooden's arrest or Christophers. Passing through the crown and making her way inside the station, she was quickly asked by Sheriff Harper to meet her back in his office. Brenda had a feeling she was about to be questioned about the leak of the arrests, even though she knew it was not her.

"What's up Sheriff?" Brenda quickly questioned the Sheriff.

"Detective, may I call you Brenda?" Sheriff Harper asked.

"Of course, Sir. May I ask why you called me back to your office?"

"Brenda, as you are aware, the news of Mr. Wooden and Christophers arrests have been leaked to the paper. I asked you back here to ask if you knew who the leak was?"

"No, Sir. I can tell you it was not leaked by me. I have never released information about a case, cold or currently working, in my life. I respect the process of the law. I have not been here in Whispering Pines long enough to know all the officers you have working here to suggest any of them leaked the arrests."

"Thank you for your honesty. Now, I will be honest with you. I would like for what I'm about to tell you to stay between us. I am the leak and the reason I am telling you this is because I want to tell you why I leaked their arrests. I saw how hard you fought to help Christopher get a fair chance out of the situation and since D.A. Parker was not willing to play ball with me, I felt the only way Mr. Wooden would get a fair trial was if it was not tried in Whispering Pines. My thought process was if the news got out early enough, the D.A. would have no choice but to ask for a change of venue for the trial. Now, I need you to know I didn't do this because I am trying to get Mr. Wooden a way for a not guilty verdict, it's only because I do not want him to have any reason to appeal his verdict. Any good attorney could see how the residents are reacting to just the news of the arrests and may not be able to remain impartial during a trial," Sheriff Harper explained his position to Brenda.

Brenda's feeling of the leak was corroborated by what Sheriff Harper told her. Knowing the Sheriff did what he did to make sure Mr. Wooden would stay in jail, if convicted, and not have his verdict overturned, she told her Sheriff Harper was telling her the truth. She was in the DA's office when the Sheriff was turned on for his request of a change of venue and understood his state of mind at the time and felt he did the right thing.

"Thank you, Sheriff, for letting me know of your actions. I can appreciate what you did to ensure a fair trial for Mr. Wooden, which is a right of all citizens of the United States. You can trust me when I say I will keep this between us and never speak of it again. I have your back, Sheriff.

Sheriff Harper was thankful for Brenda's guarantee of her silence. He finished their meeting reassuring her he would answer any questions regarding the leak, the D.A. may have for him, and he would never put her in a situation to have to lie to a D.A. Once he felt Brenda felt okay about the new situation, she told her she should take the rest of the day off to spend with her son, Dalton.

Brenda was relieved the Sheriff took ownership of the leak and a promise to shield her and the other officers from having to lie to a D.A. She decided to take the Sheriff's offer and went home to see her son. She was ready to let the day wash behind, for the rest of the day at least.

After Brenda went home, Sheriff Harper decided it was time to give the people of Whispering Pines something so they would disband and go home for the day. He had already spoken to June, Davie's mother and was informed of Davies upcoming funeral, so he walked out of the station doors and the crowd came to an immediate hush. Sheriff Harper stood there a moment before speaking to the crowd.

"Residents of Whispering Pines, let me clarify a few things about the article you read in the paper this morning. I will confirm Mr. Wooden was arrested for the murder of David Youngblood, which took place over ten years ago, and his son Christopher was as well. Christopher has been released from our custody until such time if we are asked to arrest him again, but he is a free man right now. Mr. Wooden, on the other hand, is not a free man. He will be charged with a crime in court, in front of the judge to see if he will be granted bond or not. Depending on the outcome of his arraignment, he could be released on bond or denied bond and remain in police custody until his trial. That is all the information I am at liberty to say currently about Mr. Wooden or Christopher. Now I would like to move on to another matter. I have spoken to June Youngblood, David's mother, and she has informed me Davie's funeral services will be held this weekend at Johnson Funeral Home at three o'clock. If any of you are so included to show your respects to this grieving mother and her deceased son, please do so. Davie's murder is going to take Whispering Pines some time to get past, but we can do it. Just remember this, just because you think children are being children, take a step back and put yourself in the other child's position before assuming everything will be all right later. As you should learn from this case, not everything is as it seems," Sheriff Harper ended his statement to the residents and encouraged them to go home and reflect on the actions of a Whisper Pine's respected resident, before going back into the station.

Chapter 12

A New Beginning

Saturday rolled around, which was the day for Davie's funeral services to be held. Brenda woke up early because she felt, even though she didn't know Davie personally, she had gotten to know him very well during her investigation. Brenda had a vision of Davie being a kind and loving child who wanted to be himself, but living in a small town he never had an opportunity to do so. She saw a child who was bullied, beaten, and alienated just because he was different from the other children. She was pained by Davie not being allowed to be his true self, but instead forced to live a lie to appease the masses, which was unfair for any child to have to do.

Brenda arose out of bed, put on her robe, walked into the kitchen, and started brewing a pot of coffee. As the coffee percolated, she continued her routine of making breakfast for Dalton and herself. It was a somber morning which Brenda enjoyed. She loved cooking breakfast on a dark morning knowing she was alive to enjoy such a day. She learned a long time ago, when she first started in law enforcement, not everyone has the same opportunities she had, so she cherished moments like the one that day. Being able to enjoy breakfast with her loving son gave her hope for the days to come.

Brenda finished getting breakfast ready a few minutes before Dalton was up and in the kitchen with her. She glanced over at Dalton and gave him a loving smile which he immediately responded with a smile of his own.

"Good morning, Dalton, how did you sleep?"

"You know me, I can sleep through anything and good morning to you as well, mother."

Dalton took a seat at their small table and waited until Brenda had breakfast set on the table. Once everything was in its place and Brenda took her seat, they both bowed their heads, said grace before eating. They were silent at first as they put eggs, bacon, biscuits with gravy, on their plates and ate a little before any conversation.

"Dalton, may I ask you a question?"

"Of course, mom. What's on your mind this morning?"

Brenda took a deep breath before speaking again, trying to relax herself for what she was about to ask.

"Dalton, have you ever bullied any kid at school? Not just here, but even at your last school?"

"Mom, seriously? You think I would bully another kid? You taught me better than that. If I see another kid being bullied, I am the first person who will stand up to defend the kid. Bullies have no place in my group of friends. Why do you ask?" Dalton could tell his mother was having a tough time with the question.

"It's just this last case made me stop and think about if I did the right thing by moving us out here to Whispering Pines. I learned how in the past many kids could be cruel here and even their parents as well. I know you have always been a great kid and I have recently been afraid if you could change who you are because of pressure from other students, or even teachers here," Brenda confessed to her son.

"Mom, you taught me to respect all others and to stand up for those who can't. I will never stop doing that. I also know you will not change living here either. You have always followed the law and you would never let anyone, or any town, change you because of their power or position in a community," Dalton reassured his mother he believed in her, and she should believe in herself as well.

"Thank you, Dalton. I needed to hear that today and I appreciate you so much. Would you come with me to David Youngbloods services today?" Brenda needed her son for support that evening.

"I would never let you go alone to Davie's funeral service. I think it is great you are going to show support for him and his mother, so I will be there to support you," Dalton happily agreed to attend with her.

With breakfast over, Brenda told Dalton she would take care of the dishes, even though they were part of his chores. She was feeling grateful to have such a wonderful son, she wanted to give him a break for the day.

Brenda finished cleaning up the table and dishes before going back into her room to get ready for the day. She knew she had time before the services, but she also wanted to get there a little early, in fear June, Davies mother, would be there all alone. Brenda feared the way the town treated Davie, when he was alive, would not feel inclined to attend his funeral, so she would make sure June had her there for support.

Brenda took a long hot bath before getting dressed for the day. She had a black funeral dress laid out on her bed she was going to wear for the day. In her line of work, Brenda had attended her fair share of funerals, many of those funerals were for parents of cases she had solved in the past. Even though she had been to so many services, they never got any easier for her. Brenda spent the rest of the day cleaning her house and running a few errands around town before returning home to put on her funeral dress.

With the service time approaching, she called for Dalton to meet her at the car when he was ready. She only had to wait a minute before Dalton walked out of the house in his black suit. Brenda thought he looked so handsome, so she smiled at him again with pride. Dalton jumped into the car, and they headed to Johnson Funeral Home.

As they drove through town, Brenda noticed the shops on the town square were not particularly busy for a Saturday, which was unusual for Whispering Pines on any given day.

When they arrived at Johnson Funeral Home, they both gasped at the sight of all the vehicles already parked out in front of it. Cars filled the small parking lot and even lined the streets, leaving Brenda to have to park far away from the building. She could not believe the number of people attending Davie's services. It shocked her to see such a sight, she never expected so many people to attend. The sight gave her hope Whispering Pines was able to come together as a real community.

Brenda parked her car, and they both began their walk to the service building. As they walked down the sidewalk on first street, the sun began to shine bright while birds were chirping. Brenda grabbed Dalton by the arm, as he escorted her to the entrance. Dalton moved aside to let Brenda enter first and he followed her inside the building all the way to the front of the seating area, where June was sitting. June had called Brenda the day before and asked if she would sit with her during the service, which Brenda agreed.

As they both approached June's position, as soon as she noticed it was Brenda standing in front of her, she stood up and embraced in her open arms and hugged her for a moment. Then June looked over at Dalton and gave him a hug as well, she was so happy they both could make it. After the hugs were completed, Brenda and Dalton took their seats next to June and waited for the services to begin.

During the service, Brenda could feel the love and sorrow in the room building. Many of Davie's earlier classmates stood up and gave their happy memories of Davie growing up and apologizing to June for not taking up for Davie during high school, and for the parts they played in the bullying. You could hear the sincerity in their voices as they spoke through their tears. Brenda could tell June appreciated all the good things said about Davie. Tears flowed throughout the entire room and from outside of the building, from the guests who could not fit inside for the service. There were hundreds of town folk at Davie's service, along with classmates of Daltons.

Davie's services went on for over an hour because of the number of people who stood up and spoke to June about Davie. The Davie they remembered and loved growing up. Brenda could tell hearing all those nice stories about Davie was helping June accepting he was gone forever and was the beginning of the healing process she would be going throw for years to come.

Brenda thought back about all the services she had attended and realized Davies service was the largest she had ever attended. She had never been to a funeral service where the entire town showed up. Tears began to flow down her face as they took in all the love and support the town was giving June during such a horrific time in her life.

Noticing his mother was crying, Dalton reached into his pocket and pulled a pocket square to hand over to Brenda. Seeing what her son was offering her made Brenda cry even harder. She could never imagine having to go through life without Dalton, while being reminded that was exactly what June was going to have to do moving forward.

As the services ended, June took a moment to speak to the crowd of people sitting and standing in front of her. As June took front and center of the room before she began to speak a hush grew over the crowd.

Standing in a silent room crowded with all her neighbors and friends, June spoke from her heart. She assured everyone in attendance she felt no ill will towards anyone and accepted all their apologies. Near the end of her speech, June closed with some final words for the town.

"I hope my Davie's death was an eyeopener for all the things which led up to this moment. My only hope now is that the community can begin healing and take more thought on how the children of Whispering Pines are treating other students. I believe we, as parents, should be more mindful of our own actions, as well as our children's actions. You never know, you could just save a life of a child by reacting to allegations of mistreatment of any child. Whether you hear something about your child doing something wrong to another child, or someone mistreating your child, I beg you to reach out to your child to find out if what is being said is true and speak to the other child's parents about it. Don't let my son's death be in vain, but more of a learning opportunity on how to keep all the children of Whispering Pines safe. Thank you," June concluded her speech to the town with tearful eye and hope in her heart.

Brenda could see the towns reactions to what June has said, knowing they all could have done better as children, or parents. If people would have listened to June when she reported Davie being assaulted by other students, maybe her son could have been saved. All it takes is for a parent to be involved in their child's life, the good and bad, and respond accordingly.

The crowd inside the room began to exit first, leaving June inside with Davie's remains, giving her some private time alone with him to say her goodbye. After the room was empty, June began to make her exit so she could continue to the cemetery to have a private burial of Davie. As she neared the building exit, she looked up and saw the people who were in attendance did not leave. Everyone who was in attendance had formed a line from the entry door all the way to a car down the street, which was waiting for June to be taken to the cemetery.

June was in total shock because she was not aware of how many people were in attendance of Davie's service. She only saw the people inside with many seated or standing, she had no idea there were people outside the venue until she exited. Everyone in line took a moment to bow their heads as June walked by, as they paid their respects to her and Davie. Seeing of the people there, June held her head up high, not only for herself, but for Davie as well. As she walked past the people, they noticed she was wearing a small rainbow pin on her collar, showing the pride her son would never get to experience. She wanted the town to know she was, and always will be, proud of her son, even if he was different and no one could take that away from her.

The pride June shown the town gave them exactly what it needed for Whispering Pines to start over with a new beginning, to become a town where everyone could be themselves and treated with respect.

June arrived at the car which was waiting on her and got in so she could finally put her son to rest. Once she was ready for the ride to the cemetery, the car turned around and headed back in the direction of Johnson Funeral Home so she could see all the people again. As she rode by the crowd, they all stopped and bowed their heads once more, until she had passed every one of them.

After Davie's service Brenda went home to reflect on what she had learned about the small town. As she drove home, she kept replaying everything she did during her investigation. After reading all the reports completed during the initial investigation, speaking to the teachers, and previous classmates of Davie, she learned a lot about a small town she was not previously aware of. She learned things were not always as they seemed. Respectable members of the town could commit crimes with little or no repercussions, which upset her in a way she could not describe. In the beginning of her investigation, she felt a town like Whispering Pines could never change. However, her feeling changed about Whispering Pines after Davies services and June's resilience.

Brenda felt a small town should be the type of place where people would help a neighbor when in need and not try to remain above the law. After Davie's service she began to feel things just might change in Whispering Pines and that gave her comfort.

Robert Starnes

Chapter 13

Whispering Pines Echoes

The new venue for the trial of Mr. Wooden was moved to one town over from Whispering Pines. Fearing the leaked information so early after his arrest would make it impossible for him to get a fair trial, D.A. Parker put in a request for a change of venue which was granted.

Mr. Wooden's trial was to be moved to a town a little larger than Whispering Pines, Coyote Bluff, that only had around 15,000 residents. Coyote Bluff was only thirty-two miles from Whispering Pines and D.A. Parks felt Mr. Wooden could get a fair trial with the jury pool they had in Coyote Bluff. His court date was set two months away and D.A. Parks knew he had some challenges coming up with jury selection. He also knew he had to make sure Detective Wisely would be prepared for the trial, along with the witnesses she had uncovered during her investigation.

A month passed before he was able to meet with Brenda to go over her testimony for the trial. They met at his office in Whispering Pines, along with the other witnesses she spoke to during her investigation. The witnesses included Sara, Mr. Stillman, Ms. Carter, and Mr. Brown.

"Detective Wisely, have you spoken to the witness to make sure the stories they told you are in fact what they are still planning on telling in court?" D.A. Parks asks Brenda.

"Yes, I have spoken to them all and they are planning to tell the truth about Davie and Mr. Wooden. They have not changed anything in what they originally told me during my investigation," Brenda reassures D.A. Parks.

After taking the day to speak to Detective Wisely and the other witness and is satisfied with how they will present themselves during the trial, he stops for the day, releasing everyone to go home until the trial starts.

Everyone leaves and goes home to begin their wait until the day they must be present at Mr. Wooden's trial to testify.

Before Brenda heads home, she decides to check in with the Sheriff to see if she is needed for anything more for the day. Sheriff Harper informs Brenda she is clear to go home, so she calls Dalton to inform him she is heading home and wanted to see if he wanted anything special for dinner. Dalton tells Brenda he would prepare dinner for her. Brenda was surprised at Dalton's offer to cook dinner, but she decided to let him take care of it.

When Brenda made it home, she was completely caught off guard when she walked in her house to see

Dalton had made a Cesar salad, baked potatoes, and steaks cooked on the grill outback. She could not have asked for a better dinner than what Dalton had prepared. She set all her work baggage down on the couch and went straight to the dinner table.

Once Brenda and Dalton were both settled at the dining room table, Dalton began to make small talk with his mom. He asked questions about how her day was and if she had any new cases, it was one of the first honest and open dinner conversations they had held in such a long time. Brenda didn't want the night to end.

Once dinner was over, Dalton told Brenda he would do the dishes and asked her to go ahead and head to her room, take a long, hot bath or shower, then get ready for bed.

Brenda had no idea exactly what she did to deserve such an effortless night, but she was in no position to argue. She left Dalton in the kitchen and went to her room. She did as Dalton suggested and went to bed.

Things were so good between Brenda and Dalton the rest of the month, all the way up to the beginning of Mr. Wooden's trial. Dalton was worried about his mother having to testify in a murder trial, which she had never done in Atlanta before moving to Whispering Pines. He was worried about what could happen to her if Mr. Wooden was found innocent. He wondered if Mr. Wooden would come after his mother for arresting him and charging him with Davie's murder. He never let his mother know of his feelings because he did not want to worry her with her upcoming testimony in the trial of Mr. Wooden.

Mr. Wooden's trial began in Coyote Bluff on the date picked by the Judge of the trial. Brenda and the witnesses were ready for their day in court.

The trial went on for several months before a verdict was reached. Mr. Wooden was found guilty of first-degree murder, endangering a child, hindering prosecution, and giving false information to the police during an investigation. He was sentenced to life in prison without the possibility of parole.

With the conviction of Mr. Wooden reaching town, it was as if a dark cloud was removed from the small town of Whispering Pines. The town folk seemed to be accepting of his sentencing and felt the town was better off not having a murderer loose on their streets.

Christopher, on the other hand, did attend sessions with the DA's psychologist and was diagnosed with PTSD that resulted from the events of watching his father murder his first love and spending the rest of his life fearing his father could kill him at any time. With Christopher's diagnosis, the judge felt he should not be charged in the murder of David Youngblood, and all criminal charges were dropped but Christopher must attend court ordered counseling.

David Youngblood's funeral had a significant impact on the town of Whispering Pines. The people of the town began to show more interest in the events at school. Parents and teachers began having monthly meetings to address all incidents that could evolve into something more if not handled quickly. It was as if the residents of Whispering Pines took in what June said at Davie's service. Whispering Pines was beginning to move forward, embracing the lessons learned from the ordeal.

Brenda was happy to see how things were progressing in Whispering Pines, which allowed her to look to the future. She began to see herself staying in Whispering Pines for the rest of her life. But before she could be positive, she had to talk to Dalton first. She knew if her son didn't want to stay there, she would not force him to stay. Her priority was the comfort and safety of her son. If he didn't feel safe or didn't like the town, she would do whatever she could to change his fears and views.

Brenda asked Dalton to come into the living room so they could talk. Dalton could tell his mother wanted to have a serious conversation.

"Is something wrong, Mom? Have I done something?" Dalton quickly asked Brenda as he walked into the room.

"No, son, you have done nothing wrong. I want to talk to you about Whispering Pines. Are you happy here? I mean, really, happy?" Brenda replied.

"Mom, I am glad we moved here. I know it has been tough on you since we moved here with your cold case turning murder case, but I am happy here. I have made so many new friends, friends I would never have been able to meet if we had not moved here. Are you regretting moving here?"

"Not at all. If you are contented living here, I am as well. I wanted to make sure you didn't mind if we stayed here for your senior year," Brenda expressed to Dalton, who was smiling.

"I'm glad to hear that, Mom. I was not ready to move again and start my final year of high school having to make all new friends. The people here in Whispering Pines are good people, Mom, and I think you know that. It would not be fair to judge everyone here because of the terrible acts of a few. People here respect you more than those in Atlanta because you were able to solve Davie's case and bring closure for not only his mother but also to the entire town," Dalton pridefully replied to his mother.

With Dalton's words fresh in her mind, she knew their future would be in Whispering Pines. Brenda knew she would do everything she could to protect the town folk of Whispering Pines because it was their home now.

June and Brenda continued to be close friends after everything ended with the trial. June knew Davie's murderer would never be released from jail and would never be able to hurt another innocent child. Dalton would go with Brenda when she visited June and did odd jobs around her property, giving her a sense of still having a youngster around to help her.

Brenda and Dalton had both decided it was time for them to plant roots in Whispering Pines. They both had it better than they did in Atlanta, but Dalton did regret his father never lived long enough to find out just how much better it was in a small town than it was for them in Atlanta. He secretly wished his dad was there with them, but he was also grateful he was there with his mother.

It was almost a year later, after Davie's cold case was solved, when Brenda received a call from dispatch.

"Detective Wisely, a body has been found behind the 24-hour gas station on Main Street. Are you available?"

Brenda grabbed her radio and replied, "10-4, I am headed to the scene. Can you let Sheriff Harper know I am in route?"

About the Author

Robert Starnes was born in a small town in Northeast Texas, where his journey with the written word began. In middle school, he discovered a love for writing short stories, a passion that blossomed despite the challenges he faced with dyslexia. To overcome his learning disability, Robert immersed himself in reading books that were adapted into movies, exploring the differences between the written and visual narratives. This practice not only improved his understanding of language but also enriched his appreciation for storytelling.

With a professional background in customer service and property management that spans over 24 years, Robert's experiences bring depth and authenticity to his writing. His diverse career has given him a keen insight into human nature, which is reflected in his characters and storylines.

Robert's first published work was *The Multifamily Housing Guide – Leasing 101* in 2016, a guide aimed at assisting new leasing professionals in the multifamily housing industry. His guide provided practical tools and advice to help them succeed in their new career, making their transition easier and more efficient.

Building on his early success, Robert ventured into the world of fiction, writing the *Saving History Series,* a young adult historical fiction series. The five-book series has earned him the title of #1 best seller on Amazon, and the second book of the series debuted at #64 on Barnes & Noble's top 100. His novels draw inspiration from the past, present, and future, offering readers captivating and thought-provoking narratives.

Robert broke out into Science Fiction when he wrote A.N.D.R.E. (Advanced Neural-Based Digital Reasoning Entity) (Sept. 2024), a novel about the rise and fall of Artificial Intelligence in the future. While humans were forced to move underground the surface of the Earth to live, A.I.B.s (Artificial Intelligence Being) reigned over the surface for decades, until one of the first A.I.B.s, Andre made his way to a human colony with a plan to end the A.I.B.s rule over the surface.

John Grisham is one of Robert's favorite authors, though he also finds inspiration in the works of Suzanne Collins, Stephenie Meyer, Dan Brown, and Jobie Hughes. In his spare time, Robert enjoys baking cakes, reading, and working in property management.

Robert Starnes continues to captivate readers with his storytelling, blending his unique perspective and experiences into each work. Be sure to watch for his upcoming books and projects!

Books by Robert Starnes

Saving History Series

Time Keeper – Starnes Books LLC (2018)
School Bound – Starnes Books LLC (2019)
Search Begins – Starnes Books LLC (2019)
Loose Ends – Starnes Books LLC (2019)
Final Hour – Starnes Books LLC (2021)

The Multifamily Housing Guide Series

Leasing 101: Garden Style – Starnes Books, LLC (2018)
Assistant Manager 101 – Starnes Books, LLC (2023)

Books Published by Starnes Books LLC

Novel Study – Time Keeper – Patricia Carpenter (2018)
Trip of a Lifetime – Eric K. Reinholt (2020)
Moving On From Life's Challenges – Mindy Briggs (2022)

Editing completed by

Carpenter Editing Services, Inc.

Robert Starnes

Resources Regarding how Childhood Trauma can affect Adulthood

YBranco, M. S. S., Altafim, E. R. P., & Linhares, M. B. M. (2022). Universal intervention to strengthen parenting and prevent child maltreatment: Updated systematic review. *Trauma, Violence & Abuse*, *23*(5), 1658–1676.
https://doi.org/10.1177/15248380211013131

Kim, Y., Lee, H., & Park, A. (2022). Patterns of adverse childhood experiences and depressive symptoms: self-esteem as a mediating mechanism. *Social Psychiatry and Psychiatric Epidemiology*, *57*(2), 331–341.
https://doi.org/10.1007/s00127-021-02129-2

Kuzminskaite, Erika, et al. "Treatment efficacy and effectiveness in adults with major depressive disorder and childhood trauma history: a systematic review and meta-analysis." *The Lancet Psychiatry* 9.11 (2022): 860-873.
https://www.duo.uio.no/bitstream/handle/10852/99456/Manuscript_FirstSubmittedVersion.pdf?sequence=2

Lopez, Marcela, et al. "The social ecology of childhood and early life adversity." *Pediatric research* 89.2 (2021): 353-367.

McLaughlin, Katie A., et al. "Mechanisms linking childhood trauma exposure and psychopathology: A transdiagnostic model of risk and resilience." BMC medicine 18 (2020): 1-11. https://link.springer.com/article/10.1186/s12916-020-01561-6

Scardera, Sara, et al. "Association of social support during adolescence with depression, anxiety, and suicidal ideation in young adults." *JAMA network open* 3.12 (2020): e2027491-e2027491. https://jamanetwork.com/journals/jamanetworkopen/fullarticle/2773539

Wang,Shi-Kai et al. "Psychological trauma, posttraumatic stress disorder and trauma-related depression: A mini-review." *World journal of psychiatry* vol. 13,6 331-339. 19 June. 2023, doi:10.5498/wjp.v13.i6.331 https://www.ncbi.nlm.nih.gov/pmc/articles/PMC10294137/

Zhong, X., Ming, Q., Dong, D., Sun, X., Cheng, C., Xiong, G., Li, C., Zhang, X., & Yao, S. (2020). Childhood maltreatment experience influences neural response to psychosocial stress in adults: An fMRI study. *Frontiers in Psychology*, *10*. https://doi.org/10.3389/fpsyg.2019.02961

www.ingramcontent.com/pod-product-compliance
Lightning Source LLC
Chambersburg PA
CBHW021548310726
48972CB00003B/729